# PRAISE FOR *ELEGY FOR THE UNDEAD*

"Vesely's eloquent debut reimagines the zombie novel as a tender reflection on the complexities of human relationships... This unique, intimate zombie tale is sure to impress."

—*Publishers Weekly*

"The end of the world is for everyone. With this novella, Vesely has made the apocalypse accessible in a way that is all too rare."

—Mira Grant, author of *Feed*

"The sweetest zombie story you'll ever read.... True love can't stop a zombie takeover, though it is a welcome balm, in the bittersweet and restrained novella *Elegy for the Undead*."

—Michelle Anne Schingler, *Foreword Reviews*

"Jude and Lyle's love story and fight to survive a zombie outbreak is truly compelling, yet the deeper story about watching your partner succumb to a terminal illness is what really grabbed me. So well done!"

—Sean E.D. Kerr, author of *Life at the Death House*

"Equal parts heart-racing and -wrenching."

—Andrew Katz, author of
*The Vampire Gideon's Suicide Hotline and
Halfway House for Orphaned Girls*

"Full of candor and sensitivity, Vesely brings us into an apocalyptic world that aims to steal away the parts of ourselves we give to the ones we love. *Elegy for the Undead* is a story that reveals the tender beginnings of a relationship worth fighting for as it becomes something devastatingly unrecognizable."

—Caitlin Chung, author of *Ship of Fates*

# ELEGY FOR THE UNDEAD

*a novella*

*Matthew Vesely*

## LANTERNFISH PRESS

*Philadelphia*

Lanternfish Press
399 Market Street, Suite 360
Philadelphia, PA 19106
lanternfishpress.com

Cover Design: Kimberly Glyder

Printed in the United States of America.
Library of Congress Control Number: 2019955367
Print ISBN: 978-1-941360-45-3
Digital ISBN: 978-1-941360-46-0

*For Aunt Pam—thank you for showing me
how eternal love can be.*

*For Ian—thank you for making me feel love and loved in return.*

# ELEGY FOR THE UNDEAD

# JUDE

*one month after*

$S$HE DELIVERED A long diagnosis, probably much longer than it had to be, telling us how short the time was.

"The way the virus usually works, it makes its way through the bloodstream up to the brain. Simultaneously, it works to flare up the amygdala and numb signals from the frontal cortex. In nonscientific terms, that makes you unreasonably angry without anything telling you to stop. That isn't the worst of it, though, only the first symptom. The anger happens about two to three hours after infection. Then the virus starts breaking down your internal organs—usually the liver and lungs first; sometimes it causes the gallbladder to burst. The infected body then falls into a coma but technically doesn't die yet. The point we've been claiming as death is when the lungs start to expel blood while the infected body is still comatose. Soon afterward, the body "wakes up" and attacks anything it sees, instinctually biting to spread the virus. That usually takes about six hours from the time of infection."

Dr. Cerrone sat across the room from Lyle and me. Lyle was squeezing my fingers. The office blinds were glowing. Strips of light fell on the solemn bookshelves, on Dr. Cerrone's folded hands, and on Lyle's lap. I squeezed his hand back.

"But you," the doctor said, "your symptoms are going to be much different—slower—and hopefully not painful. Since the early recipients of the drug started showing these delayed symptoms, we now know it's not a cure, but it does change the course of the disease. Lyle, when did you first get bitten?"

Lyle squeezed my hand tight one last time, then let go. "The twelfth of last month."

"May twelfth." She scribbled it in her notes. "And you were treated an hour afterward?"

Lyle nodded matter-of-factly with his eyes downcast, the way a child can't look at a scolding parent.

"Good," the doctor said. "That's better than most we were able to get to during your outbreak." Something about that made me want to laugh in a cynical kind of way. *Your outbreak*—like it was ours; we owned the deadliest ANA outbreak in world history.

And yet we had survived. Both Lyle and I were alive. We had cuts and bruises and scars, both physical and deeper, but *we had survived.*

The morning before we were called into Dr. Cerrone's office, I woke up beside him and he was already awake, staring at the ceiling, not blinking. For a moment I feared he was dead. Maybe it was a dream? No; I could feel the comforter's weight pressing back against my stomach as I inhaled and the knots in my throat catching my breath as I exhaled.

"Lyle?" I asked.

He turned his head to me, closed his eyes for a moment, then fluttered them open again as if he were just waking up. He stretched under the covers and smiled. "Good morning, babe."

The doctor's office called early in the afternoon and said we had to come in. Lyle had been going for tests every other day since we got home. Home had been quiet, the neighborhood mute, most everyone dead or gone—or rather, everyone except the Joneses at the end of the street, who had been away on vacation when the outbreak happened. Lucky them.

When we arrived, Dr. Cerrone gave us the news, the fate I'd thought we avoided. Lyle seemed unmoved—not like he was in shock, but like he had accepted it in his quiet place some time ago.

Dr. Cerrone gave us her best guess about the timeline based on the other patients they'd been studying—I was not pleased—and then we went home to live out what remained of the time we had together.

# PART ONE
*The Drain*

# LYLE

*seven years prior*

WANT TO REMEMBER back before the outbreak, before the virus, before I had even known the life I would come to know—before Jude. I want to relive it like it's happening all over again. Perhaps living again in this way is the beautiful death we all deserve.

When the sun turns reddish-orange instead of yellow, and the clouds tint the same, and shadows are flung off the high school away from the light, and you're all alone on top of the huge drain that keeps the pond from overflowing with muck—that's the perfect time to light a cigarette. Perfect weather, too: the warmth of spring after a long chill. It had been a rough year for me. I wasn't failing, but my grades were good enough to get me rejected from a third college—I had applied to five.

The end of my cigarette matched the color of the sky, burning on every inhale. I sat on the drain. Cigarette butts dotted the cement behind me. There was a strip of trees and brush behind that, and a new metal fence guarding the whole space except for where the drain reached out into the water. Burnt-orange sunlight cast chain-link shadows on my face as I took another drag. The cement behind me held the large protruding pipe in place, and usually that's where people would sit, on that cement, but I liked the pipe; it was metallic and cold, and I liked dangling my feet off the end where it dipped into the pond. The pond was really a drainage ditch, but even so I wasn't scared of falling into the water. I did enjoy the water's color when the shadows were out and the clouds were tinted and the sun was reddish-orange instead of yellow.

"How did you get in there?"

Out of instinct, I snuffed out my cigarette on the pipe (a reflex when people caught me smoking). "Sorry, what?" I asked, but then I turned and it was only Jude.

He stood below, beside the drain at the edge of the water. "How did you—"

"I just hopped over the fence."

"Uh, never mind." The drain was a frequent hangout spot for my classmates, but not usually at that hour. People went before school for the same reason I usually did, to smoke. People went during school—I was usually there—to skip class. People went after school—I was usually there—to not go home. It was close enough to the high school to walk, but just far enough out of range to not be noticed. I hadn't seen Jude at the drain in a while, not since earlier in the year when he and Julie had started dating.

Why is it that when people start dating in high school, it's so awkward? I would see Jude and Julie (God, they sound like siblings) holding hands in the hallway, but Julie would keep a yard of space in between her and Jude and never look at Jude but just look at the floor and keep walking. She was strange. Jude's hands can get clammy, so it probably had something to do with that.

I lit another cigarette to replace the first. "You haven't been here in a while," I said.

"I don't like the new fence."

"Does a great job at keeping out the school kids." I chuckled at my own sarcasm, leaning back over the water, bathing in the patchy light, tapping off a bit of ash that disappeared below.

"Is there another way in?" he asked.

"You can't climb?"

"Does it look like I can climb?" He gestured to his body, which was nice enough. He might have been underestimating himself, or maybe he was just lazy.

Probably lazy.

I took another drag.

"Can you help me onto the drain?" he asked.

I glared. "It's really not that hard to climb the damn fence, Jude, just do it."

"It's really not that hard to help me up there so I don't fall or rip my pants."

I turned away from him, letting patches of sun kiss my cheeks through the chain-link.

"Please?"

"Fine." Because for all the talk I gave other people about Wanting To Be Alone ™, sometimes a little company was nice. Because as annoying and dumb-as-a-bag-of-rocks the (other) people who came to the drain were, at least they weren't assholes. The drain was a simple place: at the drain you smoked, you talked, you chilled. At high school, you lied. In the town, you lied. At home, you lied. The drain was more honest.

I didn't care much for Jude at the time, but I stood up and flicked my cigarette into the pond and knelt down where the drain extended from its cement base, reaching out my arm to him. He took my hand. His hands weren't that clammy. He was heftier than me, though that's always been the case and will always be the case, because even in full health my body is lanky. I pulled, leaning harder on my knees for leverage. Jude climbed as best he could, clawing with his palm, pushing with his feet, crushing my hand with his grasp. I pulled him up to the drain beside me.

"Thanks," Jude said, out of breath.

"You have big hands."

"Sorry. They're also kind of sweaty now." He wiped them on his baggy jeans. His brunette hair was highlighted under the dusky sun.

I went back to my usual spot, where I sat with my legs dangling off the edge. Jude joined me. I took out another cigarette.

"Can I have one of those?"

"You've made me lose two already."

He paused, held his breath, then exhaled, like he was

smoking a phantom cigarette—except that wasn't what he was trying to do.

"Sure. You can have one." I gave him one from my pack. Being eighteen was great, because I could buy my own cigarettes. I didn't have to bum them off the older kids anymore. I was the older kid, and now Jude was bumming them off me, but Jude was a senior too, so I guess he could've bought his own if he wanted to, probably.

I lit mine, then his. The click of the lighter and the sudden flame and its vanishing, a miniature sunset.

"I haven't seen you here since you started dating Julie," I said.

"Yeah." He inhaled, coughed, then wiped tears from his eyes. "She didn't let me smoke. Said it would kill me."

"It will," I told him.

Jude shrugged. "She won't care anymore. We broke up."

"That sucks."

The conversation paused. Jude was quiet.

"Does this mean you won't be taking up half the hallway when you hold hands?" I asked.

Jude squeaked—a laugh. Cicadas were singing; we could hear them from the trees behind us. The breeze was soft, the calmest it had been the entire spring. The shadows were starting to grow too large and fade into each other. The sun had set, but only behind the trees. The cool of night was coming.

We each took another drag, at the same time. I thought it was strange.

"Do you know Danny Bridges?" I asked.

"Not really," Jude said.

"He's in your math class." I tapped more ash into the water. "He's gay."

"Really?" His voice went a bit higher, almost like the squeak of his laugh. "That's cool."

"We were together," I told him.

"Really?"

"Yeah. But he didn't want to be actually together, and then he threatened to punch me because I told Grace I blew him, so now I'm telling everyone, hoping they'll show up to the drama show he's in next week with 'We Hat Fags' signs. You should do it too. But make sure the 'hate' is spelled without an 'e' so you look as dumb as the rest."

Jude turned towards me. "That's really fucked up."

I turned towards him. He stared at me, no emotion, or maybe a little anger—definitely a little anger. When Jude gets angry his mouth looks like a jack-o'-lantern's mouth, and his eyes try to swallow you, a riptide of blue. I don't think it's very intimidating, but it is cute. I like making people mad.

I turned back towards the pond. "Yeah, you're right. Maybe I'll stop." The truth: I had never started, except with Jude.

He turned back towards the pond. "Good."

I flicked the mostly finished cigarette into the pond, picked out another, and started my fourth.

"Fuck him, though," Jude said.

I chuckled. "Already did. Pretty terrible."

Our legs dangling off the drain, the breeze caressing the surface of the pond, the shadows fading into an even state, the cicadas calling across town, the last of the sun's beams dwindling, Jude and I smoked quiet cigarettes (many more than either of us would consider healthy) and occasionally talked but mostly just sat with each other because it was comfortable. The orange in the sky faded, and then Jude got down from the drain the same way he came up, and then I climbed the fence, and then we parted ways. We wouldn't meet again until it was right for both of us.

# LYLE

*seven years prior*

**WAS ACCEPTED BY** a school close to home—a Christian university about twenty minutes from my parents' house. You may be wondering why I attended a religious school. My mother raised me and my siblings Christian, but I never took to the faith. Services were boring, youth group was annoying, and the church was homophobic. I was about as close to God as God was to me. To clarify: I fear what may happen after I die.

So I went there out of obligation: you have to attend some kind of college, and I had to attend a Christian university because it was the only one that accepted me.

College life was, for me, a blank space: a mechanical life. *Mechanical* meaning every day I would wake up and go to school or to my part-time job at a dental office where I filed papers and took calls. The job was very fun, I assure you. But the days at school were worse. I wasn't doing well in most classes, because I knew I couldn't cut it in academia, because I could barely cut it in high school, because part of me didn't want to cut it, because I had no reason to cut it. Those days consisted of: wake up; drive to campus from my parents' house, where I still lived; disappoint my professors; drive back home. The drive would frequently become a vortex, like I wasn't conscious during it. Sometimes, I would turn on the car and drive the whole way in complete silence without even realizing it, and when I got to campus I'd turn the car off and not remember what day it was or the difference from yesterday or the day before that. It was like not remembering falling asleep and then waking up in a strangely familiar place.

At the end of the first semester, I slid my last paper (written sloppily the night before) through the crack under my professor's door. It felt as if I were floating above my body, watching myself slide that paper out of sight—I didn't recognize myself. The previous four months had been hard, and I couldn't imagine doing seven more semesters of anything like it. It wasn't who I was. To tell the truth, majoring in writing seemed especially futile. I mean, can you teach an art form?

Sometimes I would just walk around campus for lack of anything better to do and find obscure paths in the woods, which had once been official paths but had long since succumbed to time and nature and the faults of memory. On a favorite path of mine, I would stop at a small bridge and watch the turtles raise their heads from the water, waiting for scraps of food; sometimes I'd give them a bit of granola bar. Moments of peace did happen.

Campus was scenic and solitary; glowing and mute. The wind was calm and soft like the Holy Spirit—you could barely tell if it were real. I was walking beside the baseball field, along a long and winding path that passed by the dorms and led to the parking lot, when—for the first time since dusk at the drain, since high school—I caught a glimpse of Jude. He had cut his hair, grown a bit of a beard, and started wearing glasses, but he still looked like Jude. When we got closer to each other along that long, winding path beside the baseball field, he recognized me.

"Lyle?"

I looked behind me, as if that wasn't my name or I didn't know for certain he was talking to me. "Jude, right?" I knew for certain it was Jude.

"Yeah." His shoulders fell a bit with disappointment. "Do you remember me?"

"I helped you up on the drain once."

"You did," he nodded. It was late in the day—campus business quiet and concluding. He stood in front of me like a wall, but I didn't try to go around him. The wall was familiar; nostalgia seeped through it like water, collecting in a calm glass on my bedside table to be there when I'd wake up. In the space of about ten seconds, standing in front of Jude felt comfortable. And then he spoke: "So, I broke up with someone recently. It's kind of the first time this semester I've been out of my dorm for anything that isn't class or work. I just wanted to smoke a cigarette. Do you still smoke?"

I laughed, one big laugh that broke the quiet of the campus.

Jude was taken aback, and I wasn't sure in which way. "Oh, wow, I'm sorry. Yes, I do still smoke, sorry."

Jude laughed, timidly. "Want to come with me?"

It wasn't the drain, but one of those deserted paths through the woods did the trick. We found an out-of-the-way spot with a rusted bench. Dusk was setting in and the woods were getting louder—it all had a delicate horror-movie vibe to it—and we each lit a cigarette.

"What was her name?" I asked.

"His."

I took my cig from my mouth, turned my head—he looked sad. "That's fucking awesome," I said.

Jude chuckled. "Thanks."

"I'm gay too."

"I knew that already."

And that was how Jude and I came out to each other.

Another cigarette in, he told me about his work. Jude worked as a math tutor part time.

"It isn't very far," Jude said. "I can walk pretty easily. It's only a couple miles down Lancaster." Which was a mile away itself.

"That's far."

"I used to walk to school a lot," he said, "and the high school was four miles from my house."

"I pity you." I did pity him, but my empathy was lacking. Feelings—in general—were a difficult concept at the time. I could only offer a solution. "I can just drive you, at least for today."

"You don't have to."

"It's just one time."

But it didn't end up being one time, because two days afterward we saw each other again and got lunch, and then we hung out until he had work, and then I drove him so we could continue talking about how *Kingdom Hearts* was the most convoluted but best video game series of all time. It was only after the second encounter that I realized how much I had wanted to see Jude; I had put all my will into the chance occurrence of me seeing Jude. Or perhaps it wasn't specifically that I wanted to see Jude but that I wanted—had quietly begged—the world to send something to change me. Instead, Jude revealed me.

I didn't dislike his smile, and I certainly had an affinity for his eyes. I know that's so cliché: his eyes. Talking about description in Creative Writing I—the one class I excelled in—the professor said not to use eyes as a crutch. Talk about the way he walks with a subtle bounce that you would expect from an acrobat or a dancer; talk about the way he never brushes his hair "because it's curly" and you don't understand how he gets away with it; talk about the way he talks. The way you speak and he listens. The way he speaks and you *want* to listen, because what he says makes you smile. The way he holds nothing against his family even though they're shitty. The way he likes it when you hold him. The way he imagines your future together. I'm getting ahead of myself, of course; we didn't talk about all that just yet.

We reached an understanding, although we never fully verbalized it. We would hang out after class. Then I would offer to drop him off at work on my way home; he would ask every time if I was sure it was okay, until finally we fell into the rhythm of it. He was almost like a best friend—in the way your only friend is your best friend.

One day in the car, I asked him about his parents, what they were like when he was growing up, how they took the news he was gay.

"My parents raised me on Cher, RuPaul, and Diana Ross," he said. "What else could they expect but two-thirds of their children being gay?"

"Maybe it was failed reverse psychology," I suggested.

"Failed for sure."

I turned on Cher; the mention of her name made me crave her music. Jude nodded along.

"So, they were okay with it?" I asked.

"It took them a little while. My mom told me she never wanted to see me kiss another boy, but she's always been over-dramatic. She's okay with it now. She met my ex-boyfriend and it was okay."

There was a pause.

"What was that relationship like?" I asked. I asked because I was curious about his ex; and I was curious about the whole idea of being in a relationship, being involved in someone else's life and being okay with them in mine. It wasn't something I knew much about.

He nodded. "His name was Martin. It was the weirdest relationship. He had a lot of problems communicating his feelings. There were just weeklong periods of time when he wouldn't talk to me."

"That's shitty."

"You're telling me."

It wasn't just driving; it was driving the scenic route when we had the time, stopping for iced coffee even on the cold days, and sharing stories about classes. I was never very good at talking, considering I never cared about most of my day, but I liked listening to Jude's stories, even the simple ones like seeing a blue jay or running into a friend. A day without an excuse to see him was a day emptied, so I started just asking him to hang out even when I didn't have class and he didn't have work. He never refused.

I wonder now if the sudden development of our friendship is a product of my memory, or if my vivid memory of the time is a product of our friendship. Friendship—that's all it was, at the time. We would have lunch and talk and drive, all as friends. I was determined that nothing more would come of it. *Cupid, you won't hit me.* Lunch does not a love make, and I didn't love him then, or rather, I didn't know I was interested. Not until the day we had lunch in the chapel, because I wanted to play the piano and that was the only in-tune piano on campus. I played the simple tunes I knew: some Sara Bareilles, some of my own work, then Jude took the bench and played some songs he knew from *Zelda*. The sound was spotty but delightful, and the feeling of leaning against the pew, deformed pastel light filtering through the stained glass onto his hands at the keys, was horrifying—and by *horrifying*, I mean beautiful and stirring and hindering my ability to distance myself from wanting him.

The tiny campus must have seen the change: how we were always together, the way we looked at each other, the way we would eat a late lunch, always with each other but less and less frequently with other people we knew.

*Should I fall in love?* That's a silly question—of course you should. *Should I fall in love again?* Now that's more complicated.

The first time I fell in love, he didn't love me back. I was in high school, when love was just an idea in my head and hate meant bullies. I was bullied all through elementary and middle school for being too feminine. In middle school, another boy asked me—my whole class around us, his small ass on my desk crinkling my papers—"Have you ever kissed a girl?" It was the sixth grade.

"No, I've never kissed a girl." I couldn't look at him, so I looked at the papers he sat on. My timid demeanor was amplifying my weakness, calling the bullies to prey on me. I couldn't do the difficult things like look my bullies in the eye or punch them in the jaw or kiss them when no one was looking.

"You've kissed a boy, though!" he said.

The class laughed. I don't remember their names now. The

tall kid with the downy middle-school mustache; the one with the Nikes and the frosted hair; the one with the messy braid; another wearing the first sports bra of the class. Simpler times, when I was learning how to deal with embarrassment.

"No, I've never kissed a boy either," I corrected Daniel.

"But you *are* gay," he corrected me.

The class chuckled. I kid you the fuck not, the class chuckled. So I went home that day after class, I pulled out those notes Danny had crumpled with his ass, I cried into those notes so my mother would think I was just tired of studying, and I spent the next few years learning to get the fuck over it.

*Yes, Daniel, I am gay, but so are you, so shut the fuck up and suck my dick.*


Now that you see my idea of love, you'll understand why I held back with Jude. It's like instead of jumping into the swimming pool, we dipped our toes, then our legs, then our chests to make sure we wouldn't drown before we learned how to breathe under water. To think the deepest love needs to fly high and free (like Icarus) is juvenile. I'd already flown too close to the sun, gone for the sky and burnt up. The burn scars last forever.

The days with Jude got longer, and with spring I found myself over at his dorm more often. We talked less like friends, less about our classes and favorite games and high school memories. We talked more like flirts, more about each other and the way his eyes were so blue and it was so corny that I said that.

"I like to sleep," Jude said.

"I like to sleep a lot," I said.

"I like to sleep at least twenty-four hours a day."

"I'd prefer to die if I weren't so reliant on living."

Jude nodded. "I agree."

Spending time with Jude improved my grades—I went from a 2.8 GPA to a 3.5 by the semester's end—but also, more importantly, my college experience as a whole. He was helping me with contemporary mathematics (yes, here is where it gets stupid: he was *helping me with math homework*) when he finally leaned in, and I leaned in too, and we kissed. It was a gentler kiss than I had ever experienced. Being touched so tenderly felt odd.

Then every day dawned into this peace, and concluded in it past dusk.

I was yearning for physical touch—that was sure—and I wanted to be certain that wasn't all I craved from Jude. So, when we were kissing a few days later and I took off his shirt, and he mine, and his pants, and he mine, and his underwear, and he mine, and I wanted to go farther than the simplicity of surface touch, I asked, "Do you wanna have sex?"

It took him a little off guard, but how off guard could it have taken you at that point?

"I'm not sure I want to just yet," he said. "Not that I don't want to, it's just—I'm weird about doing too much."

"I understand that."

"Maybe," Jude said.

And so we kept kissing, naked, body touching body, his legs intertwining with mine and our hands on each other in every place they could go. And then I asked again, and this time he said yes.

I'm sorry if these details make you uncomfortable. But this story isn't for those who'd shy away when it comes to the more intimate details of a relationship. This is for those who want to see how a physical connection, as well as an emotional connection, grew and matured out of a youthful passion; for those who want to see an unbashful love from its earliest stages. I let him inside me, and I held him as we went slow, deriving pleasure and pain from each other, from being there, from being so close to each other, from constantly and consciously reminding ourselves and each other that this was okay and, afterwards, holding each other with our whole bodies, staring into each other's eyes, closer even than we had just been.

As sex goes, it wasn't very good, but that's what sex is like at nineteen years old in your childhood bed. He didn't finish, and I felt bad, but he told me it was okay. It would take time— like most things—and we would get there, if we wanted to. I wanted to. Holding each other, staring into each other's eyes, it was okay to be there, and I still wanted to be there, which was a good sign.

A month later, laying in my bed at one o'clock in the morning, he asked me to be his boyfriend, and I said yes.

# JUDE
*one year prior*

**A**WEEK AFTER OUR wedding, a year after I asked him to marry me, five years after I asked him to be my boyfriend, Lyle and I finally signed the mortgage papers and moved into our house on a small street in a quiet neighborhood in the town of Geyer. It had three bedrooms, two bathrooms, a spacious living room, a kitchen with an island, a backyard with a small pool, and a garden space that I thought I might use someday if I had the spare time.

Lyle picked out most of the furniture, keeping to a slightly outdated style that favored artificially distressed wood, while I arranged it the way I liked. We didn't have "grown-up" furniture like the neighbors to our left, but they were in their late thirties and well-off, while Lyle and I were still stuck at IKEA, so I guessed the poofy couches and a finished basement would come in time. The neighbors had been married ten years, no children, never wanted children. Clement and

Tina liked wineries, cookouts, and borrowing their nephew if they ever got baby fever—after dealing with him for a day, the fever always went away. Clement and Tina also loved to invite us out to the wineries, and we said yes whenever we could. Lyle and I were worried before moving in that we were investing our whole lives into a mortgage to buy a house in a neighborhood that might not accept a gay couple, but Clement and Tina never cared. Clement was a bear in a shirt and cap—the kind of man with a beard that touched his chest hair—and Tina a free-spirit who, we assumed, must have grown up in a family of hippies (we did smoke pot together every so often). Neither was bothered by sharing their community with a gay couple.

"You know, Jude, my brother was gay in high school." Tina sat on our couch with a glass of red wine, the half-empty bottle on the table in front of her. Her blonde hair rested in the crook of Clement's arm. Clement held a wine glass of his own. Autumn wind brushed branches against the window; outside was the cool night and burnt-orange leaves rolling across the lawn. We sat on the couch opposite them, my back against the couch's wobbling arm and my legs draped over Lyle's lap. Our wine glasses mirrored theirs but what we were drinking was white and sweeter.

"Ricky's gay?" Clement asked his wife.

"Not anymore," she said. "He was just fooling around with a friend. He's married to a woman now. I guess it was a phase."

"Is that how it works?" They both turned to us.

Lyle and I looked at each other, eyes wide, screaming in the silence. I turned to our guests. "Maybe. Everyone's different. Experimentation doesn't necessarily mean you're gay."

"I still think he's gay." Tina took another sip of wine and then quickly put the glass down. "Not that there's anything wrong with that at all."

Clement laughed. "Tell that to the man's wife."

We raised our glasses to that. Fall nights were generally spent in this fashion.

We were a little more worried about the neighbors to our right. We thought they might be cryptids; Clement and Tina agreed. We *never* saw them that summer or fall. However, once camping season was over and their camper stayed parked in the driveway, I started seeing them every time we shoveled snow.

We'd heard someone in the family was a cop. As it turned out, Terry was not only a cop, he was the chief of police. Terry and his wife, Irene, had a teenage son, Denver, who was the spitting image of his father. Lyle and I had to watch closely and compare notes to decipher that they were separate people.

One day, while shoveling away another nor'easter, Irene invited Lyle and me over for dinner. Lyle wasn't sure he wanted us to go; he worried they thought we were brothers, or just roommates, and what if they found out otherwise during dinner? I assured him we were quite obviously partners. I kissed him. I told him we'd be there together, and so we got ready and went over that night.

Dinner with Terry, Irene, and Denver was surprisingly enjoyable for everyone. They assured us we were "much better neighbors than the people before." Apparently, the previous owners of the house used to skinny-dip in broad daylight, much to the distaste of those with a sightline to our backyard. Their foreclosure had been bittersweet.

Spring sprung, and Terry and Irene joined us, Clement, and Tina on the first winery trip of the season. We jokingly called ourselves "The Alcoholics." It was around then that the news started picking up on events in Brazil. Unusual, they said. An outbreak as inconsequential to America as it was freakish and horrifying in reality.

REPORTER
As of yesterday, the State of Bahia in Brazil is under a World Health Organization and CDC-organized quarantine in an effort to contain the outbreak of the ANA virus that began last week only fifty miles outside of the state's capital, Salvador.

She pronounced it "Anna." ANA, a young girl, not a bringer of death. The virus merited a fifteen-minute special on the news Friday night. Lyle watched it all while cuddled in a blanket and his pajamas, the lights off in our living room while I slept upstairs. He found it interesting, like a documentary from the past instead of our future.

\* \* \*

## REPORTER

The first documented cases of what the World
Health Organization is calling the ANA virus
happened in the small village of Shah Swee in
eastern Malaysia. At first, it was thought to
be a random spike in violent crime, since early
symptoms of the virus include anger and erratic
behavior. Police used lethal force against many of
those infected.

A woman, Dr. Cerrone, was there to answer all the media's
questions. She sat in a plain wooden chair against a brown
curtain. When I went back and watched the special, I couldn't
help but marvel. She was so calm, so at ease, although at the
time she was in the middle of the Brazilian quarantine, fighting against time to figure out a solution. The banner beneath
her face read: Dr. Neda Cerrone / Research Virologist.

## DR. CERRONE

While the later stages of ANA infection are easily
recognizable as disease, the first stage is a lot
more subtle. The infection begins with bouts of
unexplained rage, often resulting in violence. The
earliest strain of the ANA virus, discovered in
Malaysia, took up to four weeks to progress beyond
this stage, so no one thought to investigate it as an
infectious disease until victims who'd been thrown
in jail vomited blood and stopped breathing. That's

stage two, Absolute Necrotic Arrest—ANA. It mimics death, but the body "wakes up" shortly afterward. When that started happening in Brazil, all hell broke loose.

REPORTER

The World Health Organization reports that over one hundred people died in Brazil—some from cellular degeneration caused directly by the ANA virus, others from violent attacks by infected persons or police retaliation—before any intervention could be organized. Dr. Cerrone and her team traveled to Malaysia to research the origins of the disease.

DR. CERRONE

The virus appeared to be mutating quickly. Time between infection and the onset of stage two was decreasing. Inflammation of the amygdala grew more dramatic. Internal organs were being damaged faster. We advised immediate quarantine of infected areas.

REPORTER

Travel in and out of Malaysia and Indonesia was quickly halted. Dr. Cerrone's team hoped this would stop the virus from spreading, but it seems that the virus had already crossed the Pacific. Last Thursday,

similar reports of unexplained violence began to
crop up in Brazil.

DR. CERRONE

When we touched down in the village of Drainha,
we immediately noticed something was different.
The onset of disease was now much more rapid.
Stage two could begin mere hours after infection.
We knew we would have to work quickly.

REPORTER

The WHO and CDC directed an unprecedented
influx of resources to the team in Brazil, hoping to
implement effective containment measures there as
well as to begin the process of developing a vaccine
and treatment.

DR. CERRONE

And it's a good thing they did. The whole world
can breathe easier tonight. The virus hasn't been
detected outside the borders of Malaysia, Indonesia,
and Brazil. Strict shelter-in-place measures have
been implemented in both countries, and we're
going to see a sharp decline in new cases. I'm
confident of that.

Things we only found out later:
    No one would ever be able to trace exactly how the virus

originated. Popular theories include wild animals and mutated mosquitoes. The internet loves the theory that it originated in a government lab—a secret weapon that snuck its way out, or maybe was released on purpose.

A person infected with ANA—what we'd call a bloodied one—will practically consume uninfected people, but once there's been enough mingling of bodily fluids to ensure that the virus has spread, the infected person stops attacking. Just like that. Their job is done.

Someone did make it out of Brazil before the quarantine. That tourist returned home to the United States, where he continued to indulge his favorite vices, showing no signs of infection. A silent carrier—Necrotic Mary. From him the virus found its way into a community of intravenous drug users, and before we knew it, Philadelphia was the new ground zero.

The morning it happened—the day I woke up and saw Lyle already coming back into the bedroom from his shower, hair wet, dropping his towel and pulling clothes from the closet that looked nice enough for work, the morning I reached for him to come back to bed even though I knew he was damp, the day Lyle kissed me on the forehead and told me he'd have breakfast ready when I got out of the shower—that morning would be the last morning of peace we'd have. That night, the carnage would begin.

I showered quickly so I could spend as much time with Lyle as possible before work. We'd share breakfast and the car ride into the city, and then we'd be away from each other until five.

It was bearable, after over a year of marriage and three years of living together, but I still enjoyed coming home with him, putting my shoulders under his arm on the couch, and falling asleep in the same bed.

Lyle had his own egg sandwich ready on the counter and was just putting the ham on mine when I walked in.

"Where's the blow dryer?" I asked.

"I moved it to the bedroom while you were showering."

I went back upstairs, dried my hair, then returned to the kitchen. Lyle handed me a coffee and we sat down on the couch to eat our food. (I cooked him food, too, sometimes—just so you know.) The news that morning was the usual: traffic, politics (skip), local summer block parties, the typical Philly crime report. After a half hour, we put our dishes away, grabbed our bags, and got in the car.

Lyle drove. He dropped me off at Harrington Data. They'd offered me a job as soon as I graduated college—it was nice and convenient, if not what I wanted to do for the rest of my life. Lyle was working with picture books at a Philly press and had just dropped the "assistant" from his job title—leaving, simply, "editor." Every morning since, when he let me out in front of the Harrington office building, I called him *Mr. Editor*, wished him a good day, and kissed him goodbye.

I've tried to look back and see the signs, but I'm not sure if there really were more sirens that day than usual, or fewer people at work, or other things that could have warned me. After Lyle picked me up, when we were driving home through traffic that did seem unusually heavy even for rush hour, I remember some cop cars blocking off a residential road. A main turn off South Street was blocked too. More cops, more ambulances. It was Philly, though, so we didn't take special note. We went home, baked lemon chicken, and sat down to eat while the news played. Immediately after flicking the TV on, we saw the closed streets we had just driven by, the city we were just in, the police presence now escalating.

REPORTER

Medical experts reporting from all around the city have been telling us this does in fact appear to be the ANA virus that the world has been watching. Chopper 5 was able to capture this footage of a man running from the front entrance of an apartment building off South Street, holding what appears to be a kitchen knife and attempting to assault a police officer on the scene. That same officer later shot and incapacitated the man. We are unsure of the attacker's current status.

DR. CERRONE

What the ANA virus does is spread rapidly through the body, turning the basic survival instinct into bouts of violent aggression triggered by the smallest things. We've seen it cause murders before, and that is most likely the case here too. Scientists have made progress on both a treatment and a vaccine, but neither is yet ready for market.

\* \* \*

Lyle was watching intensely, his head farther off the couch than normal.

"What's ANA?" I asked.

"It's been on the news a lot," Lyle said. "Brazil's been having a bunch of outbreaks."

"Is it like a flu?"

"It's like frickin' zombies." Lyle seemed ready to explain it. He loved Facebook articles and the news. "Imagine like being on bath salts, but then you vomit blood and you keep going. If it's in Philly, that's a *big* deal."

We kept watching the coverage. More and more of the city was being blockaded. There were more police, more emergency workers. Officials started using the word "quarantine." They had to get it contained as quickly as possible.

Lyle watched through our window as Tina's car pulled into her driveway. "Tina's home," he said. "I'm gonna go ask her about it." He hopped up like he was younger, like back when he would hop up from his bed for food. Tina worked in the city too and usually got home around the same time as we did. I followed Lyle out.

Clement pushed open his front door, skipped all the steps, and ran across the grass to meet Tina at her car. "Thank God! Thank God!" he was saying. He held her so tight I heard the air escape from her lungs.

"Are you okay?" Tina asked. "What's going on? What's with all the traffic?"

"They found that virus," Clement told her. "They just quarantined the city. I was worried you got stuck in it."

"Oh my God."

Clement kissed her for a moment longer than it was comfortable to watch. Lyle and I waited at the top of the driveway, feeling a bit intrusive.

"I'm just happy you're okay," Clement said.

"We're happy you're okay too!" Lyle called to them.

They both looked our way. "You've seen the news?" Clement asked.

We both nodded.

Clement and Tina joined us inside our house, taking up the other end of the couch. Lyle laid his head on my chest. Even the national news was running constant coverage of the Philadelphia outbreak.

### MAYOR TEEFY

Local and federal emergency personnel have launched a full-scale response, and for now the situation is under control; there's no reason for panic. We are, however, asking members of the public to remain inside their homes until we give the all-clear.

### REPORTER

That was Mayor Teefy addressing members of the press just minutes ago. We encourage all citizens to follow the guidance of public officials and remain indoors, so as not to risk coming in contact with infected persons, whose behavior may be unpredictable and violent. If you believe you or someone you know may have been exposed to the virus, call 911 immediately.

At around seven, there was a knock on our door. Terry and Irene were out front with Denver. Lyle invited them into the living room with the rest of us. Terry was in full uniform, badges on his chest and arm, holster at his side.

Clement leaned over the shoulder of the couch. "Are you working?"

"I'm about to go in," Terry said.

"He got called in," Irene told us at the same time.

Tina gasped in that way red wine makes you gasp at everything. "Are you going *there*?" She pointed to the neighborhood on the news, the mess of police cars and ambulances.

"I won't be in the field," Terry assured her. "But I need to be on hand."

"They say they've got it under control," I told him, pointing towards the television.

"They're telling the media what they want the public to believe," he said. "It's not as under control as they're saying, so stay inside tonight. I'd suggest taking off work tomorrow if it isn't closed."

"Do you mind if Denver and I stay over here tonight?" Irene asked.

"Not at all," I said.

Clement chuckled. "An End of the World viewing party."

## REPORTER

Gunfire can be heard all over the city. Bodies of both civilians and police have been spotted by our choppers. We have footage submitted from panicked residents all over the city. Police vehicles appear to have been abandoned in the streets. We are now getting reports from viewers in the suburbs of unusual aggression from their neighbors, even unprovoked acts of violence.

## MAYOR TEEFY

Stay inside. I cannot stress this enough to everyone watching. We have already had multiple fatalities from infection and attacks committed by the infected. Do not leave your home. Do not let anyone into your home. If you are at work, lock the building down. Do not let anyone in who appears to be infected. In fact, do not let anyone in at all. I cannot stress this enough, people: stay inside.

# PART TWO

*The Blood*

# JUDE

*six-and-a-half years prior*

LYLE WAS WARM the way a coffee mug burns your hands after a snowball fight. He hesitated like it hurt him, the simple act of being there, but then he came back around, warming up. We were friends, just friends, until we were something different, and then we put a name to it.

The only thing that changed then was we could call each other boyfriend. I liked that, liked the way I could fit him into my life so comfortably, liked the way he smiled when I called him my boyfriend, loved the way I could fall in love.

I'd been drawn to Lyle back in high school (although I didn't know exactly how at the time) because of the subtle way he looks at people. At the drain, when I had the habit of smoking—he would watch other people from the edge of the drain, cross-legged, backlit by a muted blue morning sky; watching, subtly watching, taking a drag of a cigarette he'd bummed from one of the others, then watching again, subtly enough that no one would notice unless they were subtly watching him back. Sometimes our eyes would meet, and I wonder now if he remembers that or if he never thought anything of it. He kept that attitude into college. He would subtly talk about the trees and the wind and the way that nature consumes the paths around campus, and sometimes I wondered if he even knew he was talking out loud. He would subtly compliment your outfit or your hair, and he would subtly smile if you complimented him back. The air subtly changed when he walked into a room, either because he would make you wonder what he was thinking about—solemn and wrapped up inside himself—or because he would smile at everyone in the same distant way he watched people at the drain. Subtlety was his expertise.

The cuddling was amazing, the companionship was even better, and the sex was great, if not a little too much sometimes. My sex drive isn't low or anything—at least, I don't think it is. I often wanted to, and there were nights when Lyle was back home and I was in my dorm and I would think of him and uncontrollable desire would flood over me. But Lyle—he could have sex twice a day every day and still be ready for more. It seemed manic. Maybe that's what college kids are supposed to be like. Maybe I'm the weird one: it wasn't uncommon for me to go a week without being in the mood at the right time with Lyle, although he never seemed to hold it against me. I like sex; I enjoyed it as much as he did. I just had to be in a specific mood to do it. Lyle could be in any mood.

\* \* \*

Whoever changed the rules and made internships an essential part of life: you suck.

Getting an internship is difficult when you don't have experience, but getting experience is difficult without an internship. So, in this limbo I lived in, the trick was quantity over quality—to send as many applications as I could possibly send, hope and pray, and then send some more. Once upon a time, I think people could look forward to getting *paid* at the jobs they got this way.

Growing up. The horror! Oh, the horror!

Meanwhile, Lyle was a constant I never felt I had to worry about. He was someone who would come over and be there with me whenever he could. I loved having him to hold onto and sleep next to, his bright mind to talk with and make jokes with.

For all the things he said he didn't care for—and there was a lot he supposedly didn't care for (religion, his parents, his siblings, school)—he cared for Troye Sivan like the university board worshipped God. He took me to a concert once in New York, at a small, dark theatre on the edge of the Hudson river, mobbed by indistinguishable gays with dyed hair and bright merchandise. Lyle had splurged on VIP tickets (only $100 since Troye Sivan wasn't The Shit™ just yet), so we got in early to claim spots up on a second-floor ledge. Lyle was entranced by the stage lights. I looked below at the sea of people, pink hair falling against blazers worn with nothing underneath, rose petal hats, drag wigs, pride flags. Their phones were glowing in the dark, the deep blues and purples and hints of yellow of the stage lights fading, the crowd taking notice and yelling his name. And cue the dramatic fog ushering in a calm, tender voice. Lyle watched in a trance; I watched him sing along.

Afterwards, Lyle held my hand and led me down the street away from the venue. It was late but we were hungry, so we didn't want to hop on the train back just yet.

"Cities give me anxiety," Lyle said.

"But you wanted to come here?"

"I love Troye Sivan more than I hate the city."

"How about you let me take the lead?" I suggested.

Lyle smiled. "You know where you're going?"

"I picked a lot of it up when I was with Martin. It's a grid system, so it's pretty simple. We can go down that street," I pointed to our left, "and I think we'll get to a nice twenty-four-hour diner, and if we go down there," the other way, "we could find this really good doughnut shop, but I doubt it's still open. Still a nice street though."

Darkness glowed along the street that led towards the doughnut shop, which turned out to be closed. Lyle held my hand and wouldn't let go, and I was thankful. We turned back for the twenty-four-hour diner instead.

Lyle's touch goes deeper than skin—he caresses your confidence, your hopes, your desire to live. I mean that he talks about life in a way that romanticizes it, amplifies it, makes you grateful to live in the world he sees, makes, and loves in, refining the lives of everyone involved. He would never admit to how much of an influence he has on others, but he's made me happy to be his boyfriend.

You might say this sounds like some romantic bullshit, and you would be right, except it wasn't bullshit—it was real to us in that moment and in our memory, at least in my memory. It was something I looked back on when I was deciphering whether or not I loved him.

I had figured it out by the time summer was ending. I didn't know I was going to tell him when I did; in fact, I was scared about telling him, scared he might not feel the same way. There were a lot of things Lyle pretended not to care for—what if he really didn't care for me? But we were at a local farm, feeding the goats, twenty-five cents a handful of corn. I took a picture of him kneeling face to face with one of the goats. Of all things, Lyle was endlessly fascinated by goats.

When we were leaving, a bag of apple cider doughnuts in hand, I stopped, because something was stirring in that weird place between my stomach and my chest.

"What's up?" he asked.

I kissed him, and he smiled. "I love you," I said.

His face changed, his eyes widened, and I thought for a moment, *Oh no, I've ruined the day*. But then he smiled, words slipping through his clenched lips, "I love you too."

I couldn't hold back from hugging him, so I did, and he hugged me too.

It's you that I love, and neither time nor horror can change that.

\* \* \*

"I think loving someone and being in love are two different things," Lyle said. "You can love someone alone, but being in love has to be mutual, and you can never really know for sure."

We were lying in his bed that same night, falling asleep but not quite yet.

"But I think we're in love," he added.

"I can assure it," I answered.

"Were you in love before? With your ex?"

"I'm not sure. I told him I loved him, but he couldn't say it back. Later we revisited the subject and he told me he loved me too. After that, though, it never felt right." I turned to face Lyle and smiled at him. His hair was a mess along the pillow, his eyes close to slumber. "I feel right with you. I always have."

Day after day it was: wake up, go to school, finish homework, send an internship application, go to bed. Wake up, go to school, finish homework, send an internship application, go to bed. And Lyle was beside me for most of it. Lyle and I studying for classes: him rhetoric, me mathematics. Lyle and I working together on my applications: one to a data collection company, one to a market analysis company, one financial reform company. Lyle kissing me, then calming down; then we would get dinner.

The one favor I asked of Lyle, something we would both have to try at: I asked him for a relationship without cigarettes, without tobacco breath. I asked for a relationship with better kissing.

We sat at a table outside. The last days of spring semester were approaching. Both of us were cramming for exams, but neither of us was too concerned. "I don't like kissing after we've smoked," I told him. "And the whole idea of lung cancer gives me the creeps."

Lyle sat back in his chair. He didn't like the idea. "I know the risks."

"We could literally die because of this stuff. I started smoking because I liked the people around me, but I'd still like you if we stopped. I'd love you even more."

"You can stop if you want, Jude." He laughed at the thought of his next words. "If I die, hey, about time."

"Please don't say that. You could actually die."

Lyle stopped laughing immediately; he saw the seriousness in my face.

"I don't know if I could handle the idea of watching you die like that," I said.

It wasn't instant, it wasn't easy, it wasn't even tolerable some days, but we quit together.

The emails in my inbox, day after day, usually university announcements or junk, were nothing but boring. This one, though—*From: Carolyn Garcia*. It was an invitation to intern for a data analysis and graphical group, Harrington Data.

# LYLE

*six years prior*

**M**Y PROBLEM WITH Jude was how complacent he was: complacent with us, complacent with life. Not *too* complacent with life, because he always worried about the career he would or wouldn't have, but complacent enough with our love that he never seemed to worry about me.

Jude was at his internship—that is to say, he was gone and I was left on campus—for most of every day. I missed him. I wondered if he missed me when he never messaged me back or told me he was home or called at lunch. I was proud of him—happy even—but I selfishly wished he could be around as much as before. I wanted to see Jude. I wanted to see him just as much as we'd seen each other over the summer, or at least, when we *did* see each other, I wanted every moment to be as charged and passionate as I needed to feel. I needed to feel something again.

Meanwhile, I started looking at other boys in a way I hadn't before. Before Jude, I wanted nothing to do with anyone. Since Jude, I wanted to be with him all the time—preferably naked, preferably kissing. But Jude was never too into that, even when we spent all our days together. Since he'd gotten his internship and we spent so little time together, and he *still* didn't pay attention to me the way I wanted, sometimes I imagined it with other people. The feelings were small and mute; they were crawling up front—just *crawling*—and by *crawling*, I mean slow enough that I could push them back before they made me do anything rash. I wouldn't want to do anything rash. But a feeling repressed is a feeling strengthened, given time to fester, like keeping something in a bottle until it slips from your hands and the pressure inside explodes and destroys everything around you.

College is a time for experience, all the experiences over and over again until you're full, and I wasn't finished just yet.

*Cupid, what happened?*

Now that you see how deprived I was, maybe you won't judge my actions so harshly—but please understand, in no way do I hope to justify my actions, only to explain them.

Jacob's writing was—how do I put this nicely—pretentious. Snobby, rambling, Hemingway-wannabe bullshit. He was the type of guy you'd expect to see working across from you in a carpentry elective—built, but not overly; bald, but intentionally; short, but in a way that humanized him. Instead of carpentry, though, he sat across the room from me in Creative Writing II. He sat as close to Prof. Gillespie as possible, answering all her questions, comparing the works we were looking at to those of authors that not even she had heard of. But there was something about that confident pretension, mixed with the way his arms filled out his sleeves, that lured out the desire I'd been bottling up.

It wasn't a big desire, nothing like falling in love. I just thought a lot about having sex with him, and sharing our work, and maybe finding the way to fix his work. Then he could go on to become a washed-up writer—old, fat, and abusive to whatever lonely soul had chosen to pursue anything more with him. I didn't want to be that soul, but I did think about getting as close to it as possible and then leaving in time to avoid the inevitable.

Writing for me, at least at that age, had to be done in times of inspiration. Usually, that was just my excuse to wait until the last possible moment. Sometimes that meant forgetting during the last possible moment, waking up the morning of class, and looking for anything I had lying around that I could turn in.

I pushed around the collection of writing in my drawer, scrambling up the papers in search of something good to turn in for the poetry project, but it was all unfinished or unimpressive or inappropriate. I continued to push around until, getting nowhere, I settled on a piece that I didn't particularly like but that fit the parameters of the assignment.

I wasn't the last to class, which was a relief. I don't know if there could possibly be anything more annoying than people who barge into class late, sliding chairs around the room to get to the most inconvenient spot, then slam their bags down on the ground, wrestle their notebook from the bottom of their stuff, and sit there like nobody noticed. If I were a professor, I'd fail them immediately, then chuck all their stuff out the window.

Jacob, "great" student though he was, did that quite frequently. Jacob, in fact, did it that day. Prof. Gillespie had started class and the first student was sharing her poetry draft when the door pushed open and Jacob proudly walked in like he was early. She continued reading around the noise, the bag flopping down, the search for the notebook.

"I fucking hate him," Carly whispered to me. Carly was one of those only-in-class friends, but maybe a little more enjoyable than most. Usually in-class friends go into your phone as "Jackson from math" or "Leila from Rhetorics of Style"; Carly, who had a shaved head, was in my phone as "I fucking love Carly, the bald girl I hate on Jacob with." Period included.

The shy junior who was taking Creative Writing II as an elective continued to read her poem.

"If I were a professor..." I whispered my disciplinary plan to Carly.

Quietly, still trying to pay attention, she chuckled.

The class snapped for the reader when she finished.

"Next up?" Prof. Gillespie asked.

The class tried to melt away.

"I'll go, then," said Jacob.

Metaphorically, I wanted to punch him. I recognized it as a strange anger whenever I thought about it. There are people who can just breathe and you want to tear their throats out. I've known many: the class clown who sat next to me in high-school physics, my mother, and—of course—Jacob. Looking back on things now, I want to say I'm sorry for acting how I did, for being cruel to those people when they were just... being. I want to say sorry to those people and to everyone who saw a bully in me. I want to say sorry, before I get worse.

Jacob read:

> My clothes fell heavy to the floor,
> and I was bare in body and soul in front of her.
> She walked close to me,
> the distinct smell of perfume
> like violets but firmer
> hitting stronger and stronger in waves
> with each of her steps. She guided
> my hand to her exposed breast,
> and I had the urge to place my mouth...

That was where I quickly checked out. Just knowing it was his work made me want to vomit.

At the end of that *six-minute* poem (I shit you not), the class clapped. I clapped my thigh.

"Who's next?" Prof. Gillespie asked.

Before I knew it, I was raising my hand. I stared across the room at Jacob; this was a battle—even if a battle in my head—of poetry. Even pulling it from a drawer at the last minute, mine was better.

"Go for it, Lyle." Prof. Gillespie sat back. The classroom listened as I read.

### The Tacky Poem I Promised I'd Let You Read

You speak and I just sink into a grin,
Both mine and yours, now one. Tonight, we lay
beside and side. I kiss your neck and chin
and cheek and lips; outside just falls away.

The comfort sits inside my chest. I hope
it sits inside you too, inside your eyes,
a deep and vacant garden best eloped
to, my lily pad pond reflecting skies.

I used to say we're best alone. A price
to pay as people who create. A price
I found myself okay to pay. A price
you proved is wrong to set. Paradise.

Excuse me when I hold and kiss your face,
I only wish to stay in your embrace.

"Personally, and I could be wrong on this—" Jacob looked over for Gillespie's approval. "I mean, I'm speaking as someone who's only heard it once, and this is just an initial reaction." His voice was low and crisp, like a country singer without an accent. He talked with his whole upper body. It irritated me; the pretension was an itch I wanted to crinkle into a ball and throw out the window along with his stuff, and maybe him too, depending on where this critique was going. His jaw, defined and clean, worked as he talked. His hands reminded me of Jude's—thick, but large enough that they balanced out their thickness. I was lost examining the way Jacob's buzzed hair had grown just a centimeter since the semester started when I realized I had blanked out on what he was saying.

"I can agree," Gillespie responded. Her voice was hesitant and pitchy in a way I read as meaning she definitely didn't fully agree.

"And the rhythm wasn't the only thing, actually," Jacob continued. "Water lilies are an invasive species, and in a love poem an invasive species definitely wouldn't be my first choice of metaphor for—"

"Jacob, if you were writing it, this would be five pages of exposition, a nude stanza, and at least seven lines about bare tits." I only realized halfway through that I was actually speaking out loud. I didn't mind.

Carly let out a neigh of laughter, then roped it back in. The girls in the corner laughed a bit more, and even Gillespie seemed to be holding back an unprofessional chuckle. Across the room, on the other side of the circle, Jacob was quiet for a moment—just a moment—then he forced a smile and nodded. "Yeah, I guess I do that, don't I?"

My time was up, and Gillespie moved on with the class.

Carly leaned over to whisper again. "I can't believe you said that."

"He's kind of hot when you get him angry," I said.

She slapped my leg beneath the table. "You have a boyfriend."

I shrugged.

"Oh my God." Carly returned to the workshopping.

I regret shrugging in that moment. Acknowledging another boy's cuteness is fine, but this was something more, and not something to shrug over.

Carly stood with me after class. We had fifteen minutes until How Writers Read began across the hall.

"I'm just saying it's not unreasonable to hear the way you talk about other guys as a sign that your relationship's not working."

Carly had a point.

"It's not *not* working," I said. My eyes were glued to the classroom door. "I love him. We connect well."

"So do we," she said. "That doesn't mean I give you everything you need."

Jacob finally finished talking to Prof. Gillespie and came out into the hall. He was walking straight toward us; some part of me wanted that, while the rest cringed.

"I could give you a few words on your work too," he said.

Carly took the cue to slide away from the conversation—bathroom break, water fountain, I don't think it really mattered.

I stared at him.

"You've got a blank look," he said.

"I was just expecting you to punch me or something."

"No, I'm serious." His hands slid into his pockets, his eyes side to side, his calm into the conversation, into me. Jacob talked like a man conducting a business arrangement, a business arrangement that apparently involved him and me and working on my writing. "For the two-thousand-word story assignment, do you want to meet and workshop? Then you can tell me if the nude scenes are too much before making fun of me in class." He smirked.

An arrangement that apparently involved nude scenes. In that moment I imagined Jacob nude: his broad chest, his stomach (smaller than Jude's, but probably still a little loose), his body hair.

"Cool, I'll message you or something," Jacob said.

Apparently, I had said yes.

He did message me on Facebook, and we met in the library on campus later that week, in a private study room. The rest of the library could see us through the glass windows, so the urge to kill/kiss him would have to be suppressed. His story was about a painter with mommy issues (at least, that's how I took it) thinking back on an interaction he'd had with an older woman (again). It felt much more like an excerpt from a longer piece than a short story. There was no climax, no dramatic tension, nothing to pull the reader in.

What else could I say to him? "The prose is dull. Grey. It doesn't draw me to your protagonist. Does that make sense?"

"Yeah, I guess," he said, "but I think that's just my style."

"And that's fine," I said. "Maybe you can fix the issue by having his inner monologue be a little more personal. Vulnerable. Human."

"What do you think he could say?"

"Well, first tell me why you always have your protagonists fucking older women."

"They're not fucking," Jacob said. "It's just the physical contact, the sharing of touch that's connecting the characters. Like a mystical ritual, but instead of blood, it's touch."

"They're definitely fucking, Jacob."

"Sometimes, okay, but none of the ones I read in class."

"They're fucking there too."

"It's just touch," Jacob said. "Touch can be more sensual than sex sometimes. Touch in the right places, the places people usually don't touch."

"'Exposed breasts?'" I smiled.

"Not even exposed." He moved to a closer chair, right beside me. "Do you mind if I touch your chest?"

I pulled my chest away, apprehensive of his touch. But Jacob rested his arm on the table and waited for my permission to do anything else. I let my chest fall closer to him.

"This is weird," I said.

"It's just touch." Jacob placed the palm of his hand on my chest, the top of his palm sinking into my sternum, his fingers lightly spread over my pectoral muscles. The touch was different from Jude's—it was charged, kinetic. He removed his hand. "Now touch my chest."

I was less apprehensive now, willing enough to place my hand in the same spot on his chest. His pecs were more defined than mine, than Jude's. Touching him, I could feel his heartbeat, ever so slow. I took my hand away.

"I get your point," I admitted. "Just make it sound less dickish."

Jacob laughed. "I'll try."

I wrote more to show to Jacob, and Jacob would criticize it with an eye that was surprisingly on point. As much as I held his pretension against him, he was smart. Pretentious people kept showing up in my life—in fact, Jude may be the only person I've ever loved whom I wouldn't consider pretentious. Daniel was pretentious in his own way; he always thought he knew the best way to run our relationship—in secret, after school, alone. He couldn't even entertain the idea of what I felt, or what other people would feel. Jacob's secrets were deep inside, and I wanted to discover what all the workshops and the time together meant, if it meant anything at all.

I regret every time I hung out with Jacob, but only because of how I lied to Jude and said I was home alone. Most of the time Jude just answered that he had to be up early for class or his internship, so he was going to sleep. I understood, but I had to keep busy, too. Jacob and I worked on our formal poetry. I wrote a cynical piece on Christmas, while Jacob branched out and wrote about mountains.

"If I write a pantoum about going down a mountain, the structure of the poem will simulate the descent of the *blah blah blah*," something like that. He smelled of infidelity, but the funny part is: I had no idea if he was into me, let alone if he was gay. *Gay* isn't how I would describe Jacob's personality, which made it all the more alluring—in a toxic-masculinity kind of way.

When the library closed, we were still not finished writing our pieces, and it was still early in the night for college students. Jacob invited me back to his dorm. I obliged.

"I'm sick of writing," he said as I walked in. "Do you drink? Liquor?"

"Sure," I said. I usually didn't.

Jacob had a single dorm room all to himself. He kept most of it neat, spotless; only the shirt drawer was messy, to hide a bottle of tequila.

"I have to drive home," I said.

"Stay over here," he insisted.

"You didn't even buy me dinner," I smirked.

"But I do have a clean floor."

It didn't take much convincing. I texted my mom, and then I took a drink from the bottle. Jacob took two.

The smell of infidelity mixed with tequila was filling the room.

"I'm drinking a lot because I have something to tell you," Jacob said.

In that moment, somehow, I didn't feel anything, when there were so many things I should have felt. Guilt, pain, excitement, nervousness.

"What is it?" I asked.

"Your writing sucks," he said. "I really hate it."

"Oh."

"Well, not sucks, maybe, just needs work. It's very one-dimensional."

"And yours is better?" I was starting to feel something then. I was starting to feel angry with him. I was starting to feel like it was a mistake to be there, like his dorm was not the one I belonged in.

"I can't figure out why," he said, "but I kind of like it when you criticize my work."

"Are you a masochist?" I asked.

"No," Jacob said. "Sometimes I think about you. About the way I like talking words with you."

The clean room, the made bed, the soft sheets, the alcohol on Jacob's breath, the enclosing space between us, the hollow sound of the building's air-conditioning. My rebelling heart, a civil war inside me. I leaned in slowly like he was the sun, and I flew closer and closer until our lips finally touched, and then he kissed me harder than I was used to, with more tongue, more force, more hands. I had, for a moment, felt free and soaring, but now I felt hot as I kissed him—this was my choice—like I was burning.

A simple future: passion into burnt-out passion; love that never was love; not like the love I had with Jude, not like the deep emotional connection Jude and I shared, not anything like the ability I had to knock on his door and crawl into his bed and do nothing but hold him until dawn. With Jacob, it would burn out, but it would have the passion that real love eclipsed. I was nineteen, and my idea of love was young. What would my life be without at least a moment of passion? So I kissed him again, this time committing to the infidelity and not thinking about Jude. I couldn't think about Jude, back home with his family, his sisters I had learned to love. Jacob's mouth tasted like tequila. His mouth was bigger than Jude's, but his face was smaller and more angular and had less facial hair. I opened my eyes when he laid me down on the bed and saw that his were closed; I could feel his smile. I could feel Jacob peeling off his shirt, and I followed in kind.

In that moment of passion, all our clothes ended up coming off and we lay bare in front of each other. I was scared, but Jacob was beautiful in the way I had always wished Jude would be in my selfish fantasies. I let this emotional stranger inside me, and our bodies were pleased until the moment of passion simmered—not burnt-out just yet—and Jacob kissed me and held me. He held me with his hands, not his arms; not with his whole body, like Jude would.

I felt empty, like I hadn't eaten, because it was true—I hadn't eaten. I had gone home before the sun rose, only to wake up early that morning in my bedroom. I took a shower, because sleeping in the residual smell of Jacob had made me nauseous. No matter how much I scrubbed, I couldn't get his smell off my body. The shower couldn't wash away the sweat, thick sweat, oily sweat, sweat that kept coming back like I had a fever, but I knew I wasn't physically ill. No food looked appetizing, which would upset my mother after she'd made me pancakes and sausage and bacon, a Saturday platter.

She examined me closely. "Lyle, are you hung over?"

I shook my head. "No." But I knew that I was—maybe not solely on alcohol, but on passion. "Just tired."

"You were safe last night?"

I smiled and nodded. "Yes," I said. But I hadn't been.

"Good to know you got home safe. Did you and Jude drink last night?"

"Hardly even a little."

"Okay. Just make sure that if you're ever out and can't drive, you call me." I nodded, and she continued trying to tell me about when she was in college, but I couldn't listen that morning.

I called Jude after my last class.

"I need to see you tonight."

"Okay," he said. "I have to get some homework done with the math people until nine, but after that I should be free."

"No, I need to see you when you get back to campus."

There was a pause. "Is everything okay?"

"I need to talk to you."

"Okay, I'll be home in half an hour."

I was waiting for him outside his dorm. When he let me in, I sat on his bed. Between him and his roommates, the place was a mess. I told him what had happened. I told him that I'd been hanging out with a friend last night, and we were drinking, and we ended up having sex. I didn't tell him it was something he and I hadn't done in over a month. I didn't tell him how desperate I was for touch before last night. I didn't tell him, because it didn't matter then.

We sat in silence for a few moments—a lifetime passing by, and another thrown out the window.

"I guessed something was wrong," he said. "But I can't handle that. Not right now."

I sat with him for a while, what seemed like forever, but nothing got better. I didn't feel better having told him; I don't even think I expected to feel better. I just expected to feel something. And I had felt something—I felt pain.

# JUDE

*thirty hours prior*

IT WASN'T THE kind of morning you forget, that first morning after we stayed up watching the live broadcasts from the city. Irene wasn't able to reach Terry after nine o'clock. We all knew that often happened when he was at work, but under the circumstances this fact was less comforting. Lyle and I decided to call it a night around one o'clock, but the rest—Tina, Clement, Irene, and Denver—stayed downstairs to keep up with the news.

"Hey. Hey! Open up!"

The shout that woke Lyle and me might have been what woke the rest downstairs, or perhaps he had been banging on the door for a while already, or maybe the sound of his car coming up the driveway woke them and the police lights got them up from the couches, and the banging, shouting, and more banging were just icing.

"We're not supposed to let anyone inside," Tina said. Her voice came from downstairs in the foyer. Lyle was already getting out of bed, pulling yesterday's pants on over his briefs. I stayed in bed, listening.

"It's just Terry," Irene said.

"Something's up with him," Clement chimed in.

He pounded on the front door again, a steady rhythm that shook the whole house.

I threw off the covers and sat up.

Lyle shook his head at me while pulling a shirt over his head. "Stay here. I can handle it."

"Why does Terry sound like that?" I asked.

"I don't know." But he knew, because at the time Lyle was the one with a close eye on everything around him, a paranoia that paid attention, and Terry's behavior that morning was lining up in his mind. I had watched the news, so I should have put it all together too, and I think a part of me did, but I didn't want to believe it could be so close—right at our front door. "I'm gonna go downstairs," Lyle said. "I'm gonna solve the problem, and then I'll be back." He kissed my forehead and left the room. It was barely light; grey dawn was stumbling through the window; it was too early to let Lyle handle anything alone, even if he asked me to stay. I got up, dressed, and followed him down.

By the time I reached the others, Lyle was at the door, looking through the window panel to its side. The patrol car's lights were flashing into the foyer. Clement was in his bare feet, one arm around Irene—probably half for comfort and half to hold her back. Tina was there, too, her hair cowlicked in the back. Denver must have been in the other room.

"Terry," Lyle spoke through the glass panel. Terry was on our doorstep. "No one has called it clear yet and you don't seem right. You should get to a hospital."

"It's been a long fucking night and I don't want to go to no hospital!"

Irene yelled, "Terry, why are you acting like this? Just please go to a hospital!"

"Do you know what my night was like? I'm stuck patrolling the highway because half my men wouldn't go close to the city, so some asshole *bites* me, and one of my men shot him! It's his first month on the job and I have to deal with a shooting for him already! I've had no sleep, I want to come home for a break, and my own fucking wife and kid won't let me into my own goddamn house!"

"This is my house," Lyle reminded him.

That didn't sit well.

Lyle jumped away from the window before it shattered. Everyone backed out of the foyer, and Terry's fist pulled back from the shattered pane.

"Terry!" Tina yelled.

"Get the fuck out of here!" Clement backed her up.

Could we call the police? This was the chief. Who could we call? Who would help us? We were alone in that moment, even if none of us fully understood how alone we were.

Terry stepped off the front stoop, and for a moment I was foolish enough to believe the confrontation was over, but then, in the adjacent dining room, a bigger window shattered. A brick from the border of the garden thudded onto the dining room table. Clement and I ran in to catch the scene: Terry pushing out the fragments holding onto the frame's bottom, then climbing into the house.

Under his breath, just quietly enough for me to hear, Clement said the same thing I was thinking. "He's infected."

"What are you doing?" Irene yelled from the hallway.

We all retreated through the living room into the kitchen, putting some distance between us and Terry.

"Where's Denver?" Irene asked.

No one responded, but Clement pushed her towards the sliding back door despite the concern. Lyle was in the hallway watching for Terry; before I could follow the rest out, Lyle was running towards us and Terry was in the living room. Lyle hesitated, watching Terry watch us like an animal watches prey. It made no sense—or rather, it made sense like genocide makes sense, like the extinction of a species makes sense. It didn't make sense, but it was happening.

We watched Terry's gaze move to the door behind us as someone came back in—Denver. He held the bat we kept in the shed. Irene came in behind him, reaching for her son, followed by Clement and Tina. Denver held up the bat. "Dad, get out of here, now!"

Terry reached for his gun, gripping it with the force and certainty of a chief of police, though certainty had left the rest of us. Safety—the kinship of neighbors—was eclipsed by fear.

My whole body froze, but Terry wasn't aiming at me; he shot at his son, hitting him in the chest. Then Lyle pushed me from the house, out the back door onto the deck. I slammed my head on the wood and pulled my feet over the door frame to get up. There was another shot, which seemed to ring louder than the last one, and then a low demonic scream like you'd hear in a horror movie—or a nightmare. A nightmare like the one I was now trying to wake up from. The thought occurred to me that that second shot could have hit anyone, and then that there could be even more shots, but the first thought was more alarming.

When I pulled myself up, Lyle still stood right inside the doorway, turning to me, breathing heavily through his mouth. "Are you okay?" he asked.

I didn't answer.

Lyle steadied me and looked at the top and both sides of my head. "You're not bleeding. Come on." We walked back inside to take in the scene. Denver's blood was on the cabinets. Denver himself lay in the center of the kitchen floor, his eyes and mouth still open. Tina sat beside him, her ear to his neck, listening for life. She lifted her head in defeat.

"How could he do that?"

Lyle knelt down with her, holding his hands up as if, maybe, he could do something. He couldn't.

Irene sat on the floor, leaning against the counter that divided the kitchen from the living room. Her body was like quartz, pale and rigid, but she was alive. It was Terry's body that had fallen in the living room. Clement tried in vain to steady his own breathing; it was the first time I saw the big man faltering. Clement held a knife, stained now with

Terry's blood. He sat against the living room wall.

I walked over and knelt beside him, placing my hand on the one that held the knife. "It's okay now."

"We need to call—" His thoughts faltered too. He searched for what to say. "What the fuck, Terry? Why did you make me..."

I nodded. "You saved us."

He shook his head. "That shouldn't have happened."

Lyle walked over. "He was infected, I'm sure of it."

"Can we call someone?" Clement asked. "The police?"

Lyle stared at him—it was an obvious no.

Have you ever heard the sound of a dead man's gag? Beside Clement, Terry's chest convulsed. Clement scooted away, getting up with Jude and me. Terry gagged again, and then out of his mouth came a vomit of blood, a mess of blood, blood that was dark and glowing like liquid from the depths of hell. It was all the blood I imagined could fit in a person's lungs. His eyes opened, and his complexion was Satan's Lazarus—dead and risen.

"Holy shit," Tina said, rising from Denver's body. "Terry?"

But Terry's body did not respond to that name, because we were dealing with a beast we still did not understand. Terry rose from the floor without the use of his arms, only the strength of his legs pushing him up, but his torso fell too far forward and sent him stumbling towards Clement, Lyle, and me. We evaded him and let him limp farther into the living room, smacking his hip against the couch, smearing blood on the armrest.

"Terry?" Irene had gotten up from the floor. Her body was still pale, but she recovered herself enough to move into the living room; there was no hesitation, only the apparent need to confront him, to see him. She approached his back. "Look at me." He did not. "Look at me!" He did not, so she forced out a wail, pushing her hands into her husband's shoulder blades.

But Terry was not Terry. This *something else*, this *something* with Terry's blood dripping down its chest and shoulders, finally turned, took Irene into its arms, and plunged its teeth into her neck.

Perhaps I should have wanted to do something, to help her, but in that moment I didn't.

We backed away farther, Clement still clutching the knife that had failed to kill. Terry ripped a chuck of red flesh from his wife's neck.

"Clement!" Tina called from behind us. We turned. Tina held the barrel of Terry's gun in her hand.

Clement took the gun, checked the safety, pointed it at the blood-drenched murderer in our living room, and fired.

It took one shot through the temple to incapacitate it. Clement kept aiming, ready to fire again if he needed to kill his friend a third time. But this time, Terry wouldn't rise again. Irene was struggling for breath.

Lyle stepped closer to where she was bleeding out on our carpet. The blood had taken over the room. It was more the blood's house than ours, now, and all it had taken was a few minutes.

Irene couldn't speak, only gargle. Tina joined Lyle beside her, holding her hand and saying it was all going to be all right. Ripped apart by her husband, choking on her own blood, having just witnessed the death of her son, she was told it would be all right. I wanted to tell her that too, but—perhaps the same as Clement felt—I wasn't sure what was a danger to us anymore.

After a minute of us watching, helpless, hopeless, Irene finally stopped choking.

"What do we do now?" Tina asked.

"We get this virus off of us," Clement said. "We wash off this blood, then we get out of here. We find the police, or, or, the military. They have to be somewhere, right?"

While I scrubbed off the skin of my hands, and Clement showered the scene away, part of me wanted to contest the idea of leaving. Because that part of me feared another encounter like this, and as it turned out I was right, but none of us knew the magnitude of what was happening outside just yet. Instead, we followed Clement's plan, because none of us wanted to be around the three bodies anymore. With stains we could never scrub off, we left.

We stepped over the shards of the broken window and went out the front door. The summer heat was pressing down on us, warning us to go back inside, move the bodies outside, board up the house and wait until the nightmare was over.

"We'll take my car," Clement told us, taking his keys from

his pocket. He had a new jeep that could drive off-road, around any mess of traffic we came across.

I turned to look up the street and saw a familiar man. I didn't know his name, but I recognized the walk, the steady stumble forward. The blood on his chin and chest.

"Guys," I called to the rest. They turned and saw the same man, a lone man walking aimlessly down the center of the road.

"The infection," Lyle said. "Don't let them bite you. Don't even let them touch you."

All at once we saw the rest, blood on their collars and down their chests, stumbling up the far end of the street. And still at that point I didn't fully understand the situation, though I understood that we were in danger. I just didn't understand the future, or rather the present around us that we had missed by staying inside, falling asleep while others tried to escape. That cluster of cars on every highway, at every exit, in the wee hours of the morning—all it really did was put everyone together, out in the open, stuck and exposed when the worst of it hit.

How dramatic it all felt at the time; but in memory and recollection, those bigger events happening on the highways dwindle to games in a child's playroom. Like spilling out the contents of a toy box and seeing what mayhem emerges. Lining up cars in a row only to crash a foot into them. Hoarding a bunch of blocky figures, then pushing them all along the carpet towards the one you consider the hero. I'm remembering at a distance, so it feels less like the experience of true chaos. All those horrible moments feel more controllable now, as if nostalgia gives me greater strength but less truth. It's like rewatching a horror movie, where I can't change when a character gets stabbed or devoured but I'm expecting all the jump scares. It's not horrifying to me anymore, only miserable, knowing the chain of events that followed.

We climbed into Clement's car. *How will we explain what just happened?* I thought; well, perhaps the news had already given us our answer. The world knew what was happening, when here we were living it. We would never be able to fully explain the feeling of seeing three people die in our own home to those who watched from a safe distance. I grabbed Lyle's hand. A selfish part of me—a human part of me—was just relieved it wasn't him. He was looking out the window at the bloodied ones coming onto the street from outside the neighborhood, onto our street filled with mostly quiet houses, drawn curtains, people who had left or were hiding. A kid who couldn't have been more than seventeen—I never learned his name—emerged from his home and rushed at a bloodied one with a knife. I didn't know if it was an attack of virus-induced anger or of survival, but either way the blood-ied one attacked him back, overpowered him, and ripped the flesh from his neck with its teeth. I pulled Lyle's gaze away and held his head at my chest. How would we explain this? I have no idea how to explain it now.

Clement started the car. When the engine fired up, all of the nearby bloodied ones looked our way. Some began a fumbling run towards us, awkward, as if whatever was in the driver's seat of their bodies was just learning the controls.

Tina yelled, "Go!"

Clement hit the gas and swerved around the ones coming up the driveway. The end of our road was blocked by four of them, so Clement drove across the grass of a neighbor's house. That neighbor was a man in his late thirties, standing out on his porch with a rifle in his hands; he was shooting at the bloodied ones as we left. None of us thought to stop for him.

# LYLE

*five-and-a-half years prior*

DEATH WOULD HAVE been more bearable.

For two months after I told him, I didn't see Jude. I returned to the void. On occasion, I would recognize the internal shift from feeling accompanied by Jude's presence to a feeling of emotional solitude. When I would walk across campus, I wouldn't remember how long it had been, days or years or weeks or seconds, since we'd seen each other. It was like being alone in a dream yet sensing the omnipresence of someone in every corner, every tree, every room. We lived in a frozen romance. Winter came as it always had, an ambush. Suddenly there was snow every day, cold nights and colder mornings. The morning I woke up for the second semester of my sophomore year, I was finally willing to face him again. I had convinced myself I was ready to confront my wrongdoing, ready to do anything to fix what I had broken. It was a cold, cold morning.

Willing something to occur is the first step. I wanted Jude to show up. I needed him to show up. I thought his name over and over again, as if wanting and hoping would make him appear. In some inscrutable way, it did. After my last class that day, Jude was there, eating a late lunch at the same corner café table where we always sat. I had willed this moment to happen, so I had to follow through.

I sat down across the table from him. He looked up from his sandwich and his notebook with equations neatly written out. It was the first day of school and he was already studying. He looked back down at his notebook.

"Can we talk?" I asked.

"I don't think I really want to."

"Don't do that to me," I said.

Sharply, he looked up at me. "I didn't do anything to you, Lyle. Everything that happened was what you did."

"I messed up."

"Why didn't you just tell me you didn't want to be with me?"

I sat down beside him. "I do want to be with you," I told him, even though I wasn't sure how true it was.

"You have a weird way of showing it."

"They were feelings I couldn't figure out, that's why I never told you about them." I had been practicing this. "How could I tell anyone, when the only way I had interpreted them was 'I want to sleep with someone else'? Maybe I could have interpreted it as not feeling satisfied with something about us, and then figured things out with you, but I guess I'm just not that mature. I'm rash. That's why I did what I did. I didn't want to hurt you, but I did." And then the thought came to me that maybe some selfish part of me had *wanted* to hurt him, and that's why I told him afterward. "Now that I think about it," I said, "maybe I did want to hurt you, and I didn't even realize it, and that was wrong of me, and now that I have hurt you—" I had begun to cry "—and I've really fucked up everything, I'm just sad and regret it and never want to or will again!"

We sat in silence.

Jude nodded.

I calmed myself down, breathed in,

out,

     composure.

"How can I trust you?" Jude asked. "You *chose* not to talk to me about what you were feeling, and you *chose* to hurt me."

I wanted to say something back, some fix-all phrase, but nothing came.

"I love you," Jude said. "But, to be honest, I've really hated you these past few months. I miss you, but every time I think about you I just remember that you lied to me, and I can't deal with that anymore."

A moment passed.

"Do you want me to leave?" I asked.

Jude nodded. So I got up from the table, forced myself to the parking lot, and considered going back a thousand times before reaching the driveway of my house, and then I considered going back a thousand times more before I lay down on my bed.

I didn't feel frozen anymore. I felt like the ice was melting, like I could think again, like I could actually consider what I had chosen in that moment with Jacob. I had not chosen passion, I had chosen sex—sex with Jacob, sex with whomever could have come after, sex the way I wanted it all the time, on my terms, in my time.

I chose that without even knowing it. I chose that over Jude.

I lay in bed a few nights that winter, holding the two in front of me: sex and love. I wanted both. I thought: *Why couldn't Jude give me both?* And then I thought, *Perhaps he could have, and I never gave him the chance.* Perhaps I had never told him, honestly, what I was feeling. No, I never did, because I was afraid of hurting him. But by keeping my feelings secret, letting them boil inside me, I'd hurt him more.

I texted Jude and asked if I could come over, because I had something to talk to him about. He obliged but insisted we sit in the common room of the dormitory.

"Can I start by saying that what I did was wrong, and you are in no way at fault. I didn't tell you how I was feeling when I should have. I was having such a hard time not being able to be intimate with you as often as I felt like I needed to, and those feelings just built up."

"Are you with Jacob now?" he asked.

I shook my head. Jacob and I had ignored each other since that night—or rather, he'd been acting like nothing had happened, like he didn't want anyone to know anything had happened. He never mentioned our encounter at the next class we had together, never asked to hang out, never returned my texts, so I started ignoring him completely. It was a mutual understanding.

"I miss you," Jude said.

"You shouldn't."

"But I do. I still love you. I'm just angry you kept all that from me, and you hurt our relationship. I'm not mad just because you had sex with someone else—I mean, polyamorous relationships work for lots of people—but that just wasn't our relationship. You broke what we had."

I nodded. That's all I could do.

"Did you really want to hurt me when you told me about it?"

I shook my head. "I just wanted you to know. For some reason, it was easier to tell you after I'd done something than when it was just a feeling. Like something happening made it more real, you know?"

We sat in silence.

"Did we break up?" he asked.

"I think. I'm not sure."

"I wasn't either."

"Is that what you wanted?" I asked.

"At the moment," Jude said. "But now, I think I see everything a little clearer."

"Do you think we should?" I asked.

"If you want to be with other people, I'm not sure that's the relationship I want. I don't hold that against you if that's what you want, it's just...not for me."

"I don't want that," I assured him. "The only thing I ever wanted was to feel intimate with you, and then when I felt like you didn't want that the same way I did, I...did what I did."

He nodded. "I do want that. I guess I just don't express it as outwardly as you."

We sat in silence for a moment. A short distance away, the elevator stopped and opened up. A group of lacrosse players trooped through the common room and disappeared into hallways.

"Maybe we could try to find a common ground," I said.

"We could consider each other more."

I smiled at him from my chair. "I'd like that."

"I'd like that too."

Consciously—quietly and personally—I chose love. To consciously choose love, I feel, is the strongest declaration of your desire you can make. I consciously chose love over the fun of new crushes, over complete independence and the freedom to fly—then crash and burn and cry because I didn't have someone to share my life with. I've discovered over my years in this world—first without a partner, then with a bad partner, and finally with a love that stuck around—that the last of the three is preferable, all things considered. Weighing momentary pleasures, long-lasting partnership, and the ability to communicate with the right person, I chose to find a balance. Equilibrium is love. Love is equilibrium. Love—at least my kind of love—is an attentive, conscious choice.

\* \* \*

There were moments in our remaining college years when I thought we couldn't work together, but I told him what wasn't working, I told him how I felt, and he told me when he had the same feelings, and we clarified what made us feel that way—like the blank face he would make when we kissed that he didn't even know he was making.

We checked up on each other, too. If one of us had a feeling that the other was holding something back, we assured the other that it was okay, that we wanted to hear it, that hearing it now and being able to talk about it would be better than any alternative. We weren't just there for the passion; we were partners.

Trust came back slowly, and so did the romance we'd had. We lost that sense of frustration with each other. We found ourselves reconstructing the walls we'd built against each other, then putting in doors to get in and out, then finally tearing down the walls altogether.

The magic piece of paper called a diploma was supposed to unlock a brighter future. But it did not make things effortless. I would have to work hard, get internships, and eventually apply to Howard Publishing House in Philadelphia to start my career in the city. Jude and I got a modest one-bedroom apartment together the summer after college. Sometimes the mess his laundry would make in the bedroom made me want to throw it all out, and he hardly *ever* did the dishes before they started to smell, but sometimes my showers took thirty minutes while he was late for work, and I would frequently be so entranced in what I was doing—writing, editing, playing games—that I didn't even realize I wasn't listening to a word Jude was saying. And still, even after another year, he loved me enough to get down on one knee in my parents' backyard, with both our families there, and propose. I loved him enough to, consciously, say yes.

# JUDE

*the first six months after*

**I**N THE FIRST months after the diagnosis, Lyle was warm the way tea in a kettle stays warm over the smallest flame. If I asked him one week how the bite on his arm felt, he would tell me it was healing over fine; the next week, in answer to the same question, he would give me a dismissive grunt; the next week, he would raise the bite to my face and ask me, "How does it fucking look?" One week he would apologize; the next week he wouldn't.

We had to be careful during sex, just like we should be all the time, especially within our community. I don't think the danger ever left Lyle's mind, because it certainly never left his eyes. It wasn't a huge danger—the doctor told us we would be fine if we were safe and took it slow—but I think the pressure of it all got to Lyle. By our third month after the diagnosis, Lyle never wanted to anymore.

I had dreams that I woke up and Lyle was still asleep on the other side of the bed, his back to me; he was pale—a skeleton. When I turned him over, blood was dripping down his chin onto his neck and collarbone. I always knew it was Lyle, but sometimes it wasn't his face—sometimes it was Terry's, or Luke's. The thing that terrified me the most: I was never shocked. Always devastated, but never unsure of what I had to do. Fortunately, I always woke up before I had to.

It was not uncommon for Lyle's anger to get the best of him, and sometimes that got the best of me. About five months after the diagnosis, I was up early for work as always, taking my usual shower. Lyle, also as usual, stayed in bed—he never went back to his career after the bite. Sometimes I would come back in after my shower and he'd be in that awakened-sleep state, staring up at the ceiling, or sometimes at the doorway. When he looked at me, I could never tell for sure if his eyes were following me around the room. That morning, he came into the bathroom while I was rinsing the shampoo from my hair. I heard the door open and saw Lyle standing there, blurred through the tint of the shower glass. Suddenly, lion-like, he lunged to the shower door and slammed the side of his fist against it. I jumped back against the wall. He had that same stare, like I was the ceiling now. I held my breath. I clenched the first thing I could find, a bottle of shampoo.

"I need to shower," Lyle said. His voice was calm but groggy, his morning voice.

Slowly, I considered what I could say to him. I was scared of saying the wrong thing. "Why did you do that?" I asked.

Lyle placed his forehead against the shower door. I heard a shift in his breathing. He was crying. "I need to shower," he repeated. I didn't say anything, just held onto that bottle of shampoo like it could defend me. I knew it couldn't possibly hurt anyone or anything, but maybe that's why I didn't break off the handrail and hold it ready to crack open his skull; I still didn't want to hurt Lyle.

He opened the shower door and failed to acknowledge me, just looked into the dead space below us, but he did take a moment to acknowledge the container of shampoo in my fist. His breathing intensified. I thought for a moment he was going to lunge at me—I was, for the first time, genuinely terrified of Lyle—but he only continued to cry, or rather he sobbed.

Clothed in his pajamas, Lyle stepped into the shower. I made room for him, and he continued to weep under the water. "I'm so sorry," he said.

I looked at him, afraid to touch him, but fear turned quickly to pity—pity for him, pity for myself, pity for us. I hugged him, held him with every bit of courage I had for the both of us.

Lyle's fist had left a crack in the shower door.

Lyle only hurt me once—deeper than my flesh—six months after the diagnosis.

I came home from work and heard Lyle in the kitchen. After the outbreak I'd fixed both shattered windows, ripped out the rugs, replaced the furniture, and repainted the whole main floor. They always say you can't paint over blood, but hard enough scraping followed by enough coats can cover up anything—except for memories. I placed my bag down at the foot of the steps, hung my coat in the closet (every winter now seemed to be getting colder), undid my top button, and went to say hello. Lyle was standing over the stove, looking into a pot of water boiling over a high flame. Steam was rising into his face.

"Lyle?" I asked for his attention. He didn't give it to me. Six months after the diagnosis, I knew to be careful during his episodes. I knew that what made him human was fragile, and his episodes were becoming more frequent. Most of the time I let him be, left him alone until he came back and called for me. This time, with all that steam in his face, I felt the urge to intervene.

I turned off the flame and placed my hands on his shoulder and hip, gently pulling him away from the stove. His face didn't react. His eyes were irritated, red and running. He blinked when I had him in the center of the kitchen, but it was more than a blink. It was a change of disposition. Lyle lunged away from me, back to the stove. He grabbed the pot, and that's when I knew to get out of the way.

I ducked in time for the pot of boiled water to go over my head, but it spilled along the floor and down my arm. The scalding sting was easy to ignore as I watched Lyle lose all self-control. Mere loss of temper would not be an accurate description. He swiped both his arms across the length of the counter, pushing everything on it—the knife rack, the coffee pot, the cups, the vase with a dead bouquet—to the floor.

The vase shattered.

I ran to the hallway before Lyle ripped the microwave from the wall to throw it into the living room. It smashed on the carpet.

My only thought was to stay out of Lyle's sight. He seemed to have forgotten about me already, but he was still thrashing around in the kitchen. It sounded like he was mindlessly throwing his body against the cabinets. I ran into the office, because it finally occurred to me: this moment could be *the* moment. I had thought about it as a horrifying yet far-off inevitability, never truly realizing how inevitable it was. And yet, I had the instinct. I opened the desk drawer and pulled out the scissors we kept inside. Holding them as a weapon, a true weapon now. All I hoped was that Lyle would not come near me.

I stood in the door of the office where I had a view of the living room. In the kitchen around the corner, Lyle was now quiet. I hoped that was it.

But it wouldn't be that easy. We'd lived six months on stolen time.

Footsteps padded on the tile floor of the kitchen, creaked across the living room, and stopped. Lyle watched me for a moment, like a predator. He held a kitchen knife.

My heart sank past my stomach to my feet and dissolved. The little pieces left over floated to my head. Scenes from our life together played in my mind: the meeting at the drain, lunch at the university, our wedding. I watched him step, slowly, across the room with clouded red eyes. I clutched the scissors and ran.

I ran through the foyer and about halfway up the stairs. Lyle followed but stopped at the bottom.

I pleaded, "Lyle, please stop."

Instead, he rushed at me, brandishing the knife. I couldn't raise the scissors. I steadied myself with the railing and kicked Lyle's chest as hard as I could, knocking him back down the stairs. I was too busy being worried, as he fell, and then relieved, when he caught himself before smashing his head, to worry much about the cut on my own leg from the knife—not a big cut, but a cut all the same.

I ran down past Lyle as quickly as I could. He was still shaking off the fall when I made it through the living room into the kitchen. In the kitchen, everything that could have been destroyed, was—doors ripped from the cabinets, the floor covered with shattered glass, water streaking the wall. My arm burned. *Lyle would never have done that*, I thought. This wasn't Lyle. This monster, this husk of my husband, was destroying our lives, destroying everything we had built, destroying the lives of our neighbors, destroying our community, and our community's disaster had destroyed the peace of the entire world.

Lyle—the husk of Lyle—walked back into the kitchen, still holding the knife.

I demanded, "Put it down."

"Why?" it asked.

"Put it down."

Instead, it tried to rush at me, but I stood my ground, dropping the scissors. I wasn't afraid. I lifted my fist to meet him, and in just a moment, Lyle was on the floor.

\* \* \*

I stood in the kitchen, unhurt apart from the cut on my leg and the burn on my arm. Lyle was motionless...but then he wasn't. My right hand was clenched into a fist. The scissors were on the floor. My knuckles hurt. A purple bruise was spreading across them.

Lyle started gagging, and I felt my heart sink again.

But when he threw up it was only vomit, not blood. It mixed with the now-room-temperature water, spreading in little streams along the tiles, puddling on the crumpled petals of dead flowers. Lyle wiped his face and looked at me.

"Your leg," he said.

I looked down and saw there was blood on my shoe.

"Jude." He stared at the blood. "I'm so sorry."

He was crying, and that made me pity him, but it also made me happy to see his remorse. I smiled. He was back.

I sat down against the lower cabinets, which he hadn't ripped apart. It looked as if he was now the one scared of me. "Come sit with me," I said.

He stumbled over and sat down beside me, shoulder to shoulder. For a moment, we were quiet.

"Are you scared of me?" Lyle asked.

Rain pattered against the window. Soft, grey light came through the glass, illuminating the dust floating in our kitchen. We'd always wanted to replace the dim ceiling fixtures, but we never had.

"Please give me the knife." I laid my palm open on my lap.

Lyle placed the knife on the tile and slid it into the center of the floor, where it caught in the mixture of glass and water and vomit. The kitchen was quiet again. I placed my head on Lyle's shoulder. "I'm terrified of you," I said. "But I'm more petrified *for* you."

"I feel worse," Lyle said. He held my hand. "I love you."

I squeezed his hand back. "I love you more than I'm scared of you."

I felt Lyle shake his head. "I'm not gonna live long," Lyle said. "But I don't think I can stay here knowing I could hurt you. I wish I could spend time with you, go to wineries together or hang out with our friends." He paused. "But they're dead, and you're the only thing I have left. I can't hurt you."

I put Lyle to bed early, kissed his forehead, and wished him good night. Then I called Dr. Cerrone and told her what had happened. The next day, a nurse came over to help Lyle pack his things. She was kind, but Lyle was mostly dismissive of her suggestions. I packed the important things he ignored and left the stuff that I could bring him later if he wanted. The nurse insisted that Lyle ride in her van, but I insisted I take him myself. I became almost as dismissive as Lyle. The nurse had no choice but to agree.

# LYLE

*seven months after*

WINTERBURY VILLAGE WASN'T specifically for people infected with ANA. If it were, I'd have been their only patient, since most people infected with the virus were already dead by the time I arrived. I was the place's youngest patient when I was brought there, put on a hall with a man whose face was blotched to hell, another who wouldn't stop coughing, and a woman whose hoarse, cancer-ridden laughter was a macabre welcome to the ward.

Yet I was the freak. I was the dangerous one, who required protocols and special staff trainings and my own personal executioner on call at all times, just in case.

Jude handled the paperwork. I sat in the chair and looked out the window of my new room. The whole building was at ground level, and my room looked out into the garden. Patients and nurses were out there already, taking early afternoon strolls, the patients wrapped in blankets tucked tightly between their rears and their wheelchairs. The bright sunlight made it easy to notice their glances toward my window, nurses and patients alike—all curious to see the ticking time bomb, the curse, the demon inside me. I tried to ignore the fact that people slouching in their seats, old folks who had degenerated far enough to lose any sense of decency, were staring at *me*. At least I would never have their wrinkled skin. I tried to focus on the bare winter plants that grew around them instead; I recognized a few by their empty branches. Magnolias. Possibly primroses. And lilacs, right outside my room, a few bare branches arching into view. I thought of cutting a branch in spring, maybe finding a cup of water to keep it in, lighten up the space. I wanted a closer look, to know for sure if I had something to look forward to here, but Rachel, the nurse, was at the window before I could tilt my head out. She guided me away, hands hovering a centimeter from my chest.

"We want to keep the window shut, okay, Lyle?"

She closed the window. I looked back at Jude, who had paused in the midst of filling out paperwork to look at me. He nodded.

Once the paperwork was done, and I was fully checked in and my fate sealed, Rachel left. I sat on the bed. Jude was silent.

"I don't want to wake up without you tomorrow," Jude said.

I nodded. "Take a nap with me." Though it might not have been allowed, Jude stayed with me in the twin-size bed the home had provided. It felt like we were back in his dorm bed in college, holding onto each other so as not to fall off.

\* \* \*

Moving to the home was a necessity—and by a *necessity* I mean a selfish demand on the world's part, because I was a danger—and by *danger* I mean hardly a nuisance, just because some fucking monster had to lose his whole goddamn family and then bite me—and by *bite me* I mean ruin my whole fucking life. If I could kill him again, I would.

Food on a hospital tray, such as mashed potatoes and green-bean shit, is the worst thing you'll put in your mouth until they start giving you drugs you're supposed to take twice a day—happy pills. The pills make me cloudy, so that sometimes I can't even remember what part of the home I'm in, and I like to keep track of that just in case I ever decide to escape and rampage through town. Let it all burn with me—or rather, let it all burn except for Jude.

The drugs don't just change you, they take away every bit of yourself you have left. They were taking away the small core of humanity I could still feel inside me. I stopped taking them whenever they weren't forced down my throat, even if that meant I had to fight the part of me that wasn't human. When I was alone, I found myself screaming: *Get out! Get out of me!* Maybe to a demon, maybe to the virus, whatever it is.

Rachel would come in frequently to check up on me. She knew to stay clear whenever I had an episode, but now the episodes were getting more ingrained in me as a person, or at least that's what the doctors told me. Dr. Cerrone was there every weekend to see how I was doing, checking in on me, researching me.

I sat on the bed when Rachel came in.

"Did you like your dinner?" she asked.

"I'd rather throw up blood."

"Don't joke about that, Lyle."

I grunted. I sat up and the bite on my arm started to hurt, a sharp pain. I held in the audible expression of agony and put pressure on it until it went away.

Rachel took notice. "Make sure you keep us up to date with what you can and can't do, Lyle. If you're having trouble eating or getting up or going to the bathroom, make sure you get a nurse."

"I'm not a child, Rachel. I can wipe my own ass."

"But we're here to do it in case you need it. The doctors aren't sure how much your motor functions are going to be affected."

"So that's all I am now? A fucking case?" I picked up the (full) bottle of pills on the table beside me. "I need more pills." I then threw the bottle at the wall beside her, which made her gasp. I was happy to frighten her; I wondered if I frightened everyone. I leaned back in the bed. "God, I can't wait to die." As I said that, I felt my stomach twist in on itself. "Call Jude," I said.

"There's no visitors right now—"

I screamed, "Call Jude for me right now, you fucking bitch, or I'll bite the shit out of you and everyone in this place and then no one will get visitors."

"Lyle, you can't—"

I threw off the covers and swung my legs over the side of the bed. Rachel was out of the room before my feet touched the ground, locking the door from the outside. Rachel never came back into my room after that. Jude was there within two hours.

Some days I question: why not just kill myself now? Kill the infection, get the upper hand on the virus, laugh in its face? I could take away all the power it has over me. I could ruin its master plan to use me to spread the blight. Some days I think that. Those are the days I almost forget about Jude.

Jude, who's always taken care of me even when the nurses refuse to stay in the room, like when I get too violent during episodes. Sometimes they have to strap my arms and legs to the bed. I thrash around, nearly tearing my limbs off in rage, with screams that I hope will wake up the whole building. I always wake from those times crying—because I don't want to be like this, strapped to a bed, alone and scared and knowing I am going to die in this room without anyone's pity. That's why Jude tries to be here with me as much as possible, rubbing my hair through the episodes until I come to, then laying with me while I cry.

One night I came to and noticed Jude playing a song from his phone that I hadn't listened to in a long time—it was our wedding song. Jack Garratt. "Weathered." I think it may have been the one time I came back to consciousness without crying because I was strapped down on the bed. This time, I couldn't cry, because all I wanted to do was listen to Jude's voice singing along.

The worst part about dying isn't the actual dying. I don't

even have to try for that. No, the worst part about dying is trying to figure out how to leave the ones you love. How can I leave Jude?

# PART THREE

*The Tents*

# LYLE

*twenty-seven hours prior*

I N THOSE MINUTES after we left the spurious safety of our house, now stained with blood from the front steps to the kitchen, none of us knew what road to take. We didn't know that the answer didn't matter—any road would have been a death sentence.

Clement drove the jeep along back roads as much as possible, trying to gain ground towards the entrance onto I-95. The town was awake, in some fashion. There were bloodied ones on every street, at least one roaming every sidewalk—some in regular garb and some in pajamas—like they were keeping watch. When they saw the car, they perked up, filled with primal fury, and chased us as best they could on their jerky legs. The jeep was our life-saver. Closer to I-95, abandoned cars blocked every lane, along with a few roaming bloodied ones, most likely the reason everyone else had fled. Taking the highway south wasn't going to be an option, so Clement backed up the car and turned us west.

Main Street was a long barrier that ran too far in each direction for us to avoid it, so we had no choice but to find a way across. Clement pulled us into an intersection blocked by an accident: a tractor-trailer for Whole Foods had run a red light, sending another car tumbling down the street, where it had been left smoldering. That's the thing that still bothers Jude the most about that day. He once asked me if God could be punishing us for not taking the time to help, or at least try to help, anyone we came across—the people who might have still been alive. I told him that then we would have died, definitely. Anyway, I don't believe in karma, and I question a God who would test someone that way. I lost faith long ago in the kind of God who could tell Abraham to sacrifice his own son for the sole purpose of testing his obedience. A true God would be like a true king, with a power used to protect, not to murder in cold blood. Jude and I were protecting ourselves.

Jude didn't agree.

The truck's cabin was empty, but traffic from both sides had slammed into it. People—dead people, their heads bashed into the wheel or all their bones broken—were left in those cars. Traffic was stopped in both directions as far as we could see, and it all might have been believable if it weren't so quiet—the hiss of smoke rising from the cars, the sun-bleached grass running down the median, shops that had never lifted their gates for the morning. Tina pointed out a gap in the traffic that Clement could probably weave the jeep through, where northbound traffic had crossed the median to try to get around the wreckage. So many cars, as far as we could see, falling off into suburban horizon a few miles down. Weaving through them was a puzzle for Clement.

"Where is everyone?" Tina asked.

"Maybe someone came through and picked them up," Jude suggested.

I thought he was being naïve. "Either they're well hidden somewhere or they're walking around town with blood on their chests."

"I hope it's only here," Clement said. The thought of that— of the infection spreading this quickly across the country *or the world*—made me question if we should even be trying to escape. What if we were already infected?

As he maneuvered the last angle around the other cars, pulling out into the clear on the other end of the grass, something scraped the back of the jeep. It was as subtle as a bomb explosion. Whatever it was wasn't trying to be sneaky, and because we were in an environment that we still couldn't understand, and our survival instincts hadn't fully kicked in quite yet, Clement stopped the car, the way you do when someone rear-ends you. "What was that?"

It was our last moment of quiet sounds—the wind and the engine and the flocking of the birds. The calm before the apocalypse.

"Lyle!" Clement yelled. "Get away from the—" He was trying to warn me of what he saw in his rearview mirror, but it bashed in my window too quickly. It was a woman with blood dripping out of her mouth; she grabbed my arm and pulled me closer, chomping the air. Jude grabbed my other arm and pulled me back, ripping me from her grasp. Clement pointed the gun at my window and shot. Her head slammed into the window frame, slathering blood all over it as she slid down the outside. Another window shattered, this time Tina's on the passenger side. Another woman, another monster, reached in and grabbed Tina's neck, pulling her head halfway out of the car and plunging its blood-drenched teeth into her neck. Clement aimed the gun but couldn't get a clear shot. Instead, he slammed the gun down on the attacker's head over and over, making a dent that was visible from the back seat but still not enough to faze it until after the gun had slammed into the temple of its head hard enough to make it gush blood into Tina's lap. The monster finally let go and collapsed outside in the grass.

Jude held me close and checked my arm for wounds; I was clean except for the smears of someone else's blood and a cut on my cheek from the glass. Tina was choking the same way Irene had. Clement had crawled onto the center console to put pressure on the bite on her neck, a pointless task. She was gone within the minute, but Clement kept trying.

"Come on. Come on! Don't fall asleep, babe, don't go to sleep!"

I think Jude and I were both too shocked to move from where we were huddled in the back seat, in the center, away from both windows. For us, finally, survival instinct had kicked in, and the world outside was full of monsters.

After another minute, Clement gave up and fell into Tina's shoulder. Jude and I could only watch and fear the alternate reality where Clement hadn't killed the one grabbing me, and then maybe he would have reacted quickly enough to save Tina, and then they would be watching Jude stand over me as I took my last gasps for air, for life.

The last thing I wanted to interrupt the quiet of Clement's tears was Tina's guttural gagging. Clement stopped crying only to watch Tina reanimate, open her eyes, and grab him by the face. Tina bit into Clement, ripping off the flesh of his cheek.

I pulled Jude towards my door. There was nothing we could do for them. There was nothing. I keep telling myself that. We were helpless in the back seat, and so we escaped. I stepped out onto the grass of the median, Jude behind me. There were more bloodied ones weaving their way through the traffic, coming up both sides of the street at a slow pace like beasts whose prey was already cornered. The bloodied ones looked at you with glazed eyes, like every blood vessel had burst and now they wanted yours—ours. A shot rang out from the jeep, but before we could figure out what had happened Jude yelled, "Hey!"

Jude ran away from the jeep, down towards the intersection, where a car was approaching. He waved his hands. "Help! We're not sick!"

It was a pickup truck that picked up speed once it saw us. A bloodied one picked up its own speed along the road we were coming from. Jude didn't seem to notice, so I yelled, "Watch out!" It was instinct to run to his side faster than the shambling bloodied ones could get there. When the bloodied one reached us I kicked my foot into its chest, pushing it to the ground.

The truck stopped in the grass a short distance in front of us. Two people sat inside. The driver stepped out and the passenger followed, both holding heavy AR weapons, but they wore civilian clothing. More of the bloodied ones started to run at us, and the man from the truck shot first. Jude brought us both down to our knees, wrapping his arms around my body. The gunfire stopped just as suddenly as it had begun, and when Jude let go of me, I looked around to see the bloodied ones collapsed around us—in the grass, in the road, against the abandoned cars—a bullet in each of their heads.

We breathed.

We breathed again.

And when the echoes of the gunshots finally faded, we breathed once more.

The people from the truck kept their distance from us, bickering quietly. The woman was pointing at Jude and me. The man shook his head and walked closer to us. They were both young, around our age, him lean and dark-complexioned, her stocky and pale with a hard jawline tightened by the tension in her face. I thought perhaps they'd known each other for a long time, perhaps they were even together. But we'd later find out they were barely acquaintances before this—casual sporting events, group outings, happy hours spent three chairs apart.

"Keiynan, don't be stupid!" the woman yelled.

"Are you two okay?" Keiynan asked.

Jude and I were both speechless for a moment.

I nodded. "Yeah."

"Are you infected?" he asked.

"I don't think so."

"Did they bite you?"

I shook my head.

Keiynan looked back at the woman. "Are you happy?"

"We need to leave," she said. "More probably heard the shooting."

The door to the jeep clicked open. Keiynan raised his weapon at the sound, but he only backed up when Clement stumbled out, his cheek torn off.

"Wait, he's with us," Jude told Keiynan.

Clement stood there, gun in hand, but he didn't look primal; he looked broken, defeated, and sad. Clement raised the gun to his own temple and pulled the trigger. He fell quickly, the last of our friends, another body on the ground.

Jude held onto me, but this time it was his head on my shoulder. He clenched my shirt and, finally, he let out a sob.

And I looked at the red grass.


Keiynan and Kim let us sit in the flatbed of their truck, where we watched the decimated town pass by in the dim afternoon light.

Jude and I sat amid boxes of canned goods and other supplies, our backs to the truck's cabin. Jude held onto my waist like a seatbelt, like he was afraid I'd fall out on any bump we hit across town. The grey morning had never brightened, the clouds never receded. All day they had threatened rain, but it hadn't come yet. We didn't go far from the intersection where we had started, but it took a lot of time to navigate along streets that didn't have too many of the bloodied ones roaming. That's when we got the name for them: the bloodied ones.

"Slow down at that turn up ahead," Kim told Keiynan. "I want to see if there are still some of those bloodied ones trying to get into the Wawa." There weren't. They had broken down the window, and we saw them milling around inside when we passed.

Keiynan turned the truck into a parking garage on a relatively quiet road. "All the infected around here are cooped up inside the apartments across the street," Keiynan told us through his back window. "We're not going to disturb them as long as they stay inside." He drove up three levels, to the ramp that led to the roof, but that ramp was blocked by a barrier of cars. He parked the truck off to the side. Two men stood behind the barrier, one with a rifle, the other with a pistol and a bat strapped to his back.

We all stepped out of the truck. The grey light that filtered in from outside didn't do much for the dark interior of the parking garage.

"This place is safe for now," Kim told Jude and me, "so I need to check you for bites or any injuries before you do anything else."

Jude and I agreed.

Keiynan and Kim stepped over a Honda Civic that formed the center of the barrier, leaving dents in its hood, jumping down to the other side. The metallic vibrations echoed through the garage. I helped Jude up, then stepped across myself. My eyes met those of the man with the rifle. The guards wore police uniforms and watched Jude and me like we might explode at any moment; I couldn't blame them. If we were infected, we might. Jude seemed to understand too, saying nothing, letting them watch us, holding my hand.

The rooftop level looked like a small refugee camp, with tents set up against the concrete railings and inner walls, everyone huddled close together, whispering so as to not draw attention to themselves. There were people I recognized vaguely from town. The manager of the ACME, usually well dressed, had lost the tie and dress shirt, and his dark chest was exposed to the sun. He stood looking off the edge of the garage roof.

Another guy, Luke, was on the town council, but now he sat with his back against the wall, a child on his lap—his son? I didn't know much about his life. The child couldn't have been past the age of six. Where had his mother gone? For both of their sakes, I hoped she had gone long before this. But Luke had tearstained cheeks and heavy eyes, and there was blood on his pants. The child was quiet; I hoped at least he hadn't seen it happen.

Others were scattered throughout the rooftop camp, but not many, maybe twenty-five at most.

Kim brought us to a makeshift infirmary and quarantine. It was the biggest tent of the bunch, set up in a corner away from the rest. Inside there was a man lying on a blanket, but the tent was big enough to put some distance between him and the zippered entrance. Keiynan sat on a first-aid kit beside the man. Kim turned to us. "Strip down," she said.

"What?" asked Jude.

"I have to check you for bites. I know it's weird, but it's the only way. We had everyone do it last night when we secured this place, and we're not screwing it up for anyone's dignity, so take off your clothes."

Keiynan waved with his back to us. "I won't look."

Jude and I both stripped to our underwear and let Kim check our skin; she paid special attention to anything with blood on it, making sure it wasn't ours.

"That cut on your cheek?" she asked me.

"Glass."

She looked at me for a second, her eyes observing my eyes, and I knew she was trying to tell if I was lying. I assured myself there was nothing to detect and looked back, trying to decipher if she had really gone through this for everyone there. Had so much happened overnight? We couldn't have been the only ones who heeded the public warning to stay inside.

Kim nodded, satisfied. "Thank you, guys. You can put your clothes back on. I'll clean that cut for you."

"Are you guys cops?" I asked while Jude and I dressed.

"Keiynan's a veteran," Kim said.

Keiynan waved his hand again, too modest to turn around until we were clothed. "Barely," he added. "I got basic training, then sat at a desk for four years."

"I'm a nurse at Cooper across the river," Kim told us. "Don

and Max down by the barricade are cops, two of the only ones that didn't get killed or flee west."

"You know how to use a gun."

Kim shrugged. "I like guns."

Jude and I pulled our shoes on.

"Keiynan, can you bring that first-aid kit over?" Kim called. She cleaned my cut and asked if I wanted a Band-Aid over it. I declined, but she insisted. "It wasn't really a question. Don't fuck with infections."

"Try to be quiet out there," Keiynan said. "Everyone's been up all night, so they're trying to get some sleep. Most of them were stuck out when military blocked off the roads and traffic got too bad. We're just waiting for them to actually send people in to help us now." He shook his head. "There's an extra tent you can set up. We're having dinner tonight, too. It won't be much. Jerome let me take a few things from the ACME before the looting got crazy last night. Enough pre-made wraps and ravioli for the lot of us. I figure we have to eat it before it goes bad, and hopefully we won't be here much longer."

Keiynan gave us the spare tent, and we set it up near the wall like the others. I didn't mind us having a tent of our own, but the fact that there were so few tents and still enough to go around was disturbing.

Snores were coming from the tent beside us. I found it insane that anyone was able to sleep after being out there. I was afraid to sleep—afraid of nightmares—but after we set up the tent, Jude lay down inside on the thin layer of canvas above the concrete. He reached out to me. "I want to hold you." And I wanted to hold him too, wanted to make sure this wasn't the alternate reality where one of us had died instead of all our friends. I wanted to assure myself we were both still here, so I crawled in next to him, zipped up the tent, took off my stained shirt, wrapped my arms around him, and eventually fell asleep.

Keiynan peeked into our tent, waking us up with the zipping noise and the sudden light. "Oh, sorry," Keiynan said. "I just—I mean, was I interrupting?"

Jude and I both shook our heads, wiping the sleep from our eyes. How long had we slept?

"No, we were just sleeping," Jude said.

"Okay. I didn't know you two were together. I thought you were, like…"

I laughed. "If you say brothers, I'll throw you off the roof."

Keiynan smiled and shook his head. "I will not, then. We're having that dinner in a half-hour if you're still interested."

We had slept for six hours, which, in retrospect, made a lot of sense.

Containers of pre-cooked (pre-looted) food were laid out across three parking spaces. Aluminum pans filled with Alfredo pasta, salads, cups of dressing, chicken wraps, ravioli, and lukewarm chicken parmesan. Everyone came out from their tents and we finally got a good look at them. None of the little groups looked like complete families, and almost all of them had some sort of blood staining their clothing, but at least it wasn't on their mouths or chests. Many of them I didn't recognize, people I would maybe pass while grocery shopping or sit next to in a restaurant without ever looking at their faces or knowing the smallest bit about who they were. The few I did recognize—the Hispanic woman who always walked around our neighborhood with her husband, the barista from the Starbucks that Jude and I would always say had a cute body—they probably didn't recognize us. But we all ate the food, mostly in silence.

The food tasted like survivor's guilt.

We sat on the concrete beside Kim, who sat next to Keiynan, who sat next to a slightly younger woman, who peeked past Kim at the two of us. She must have noticed she had caught my eye, because she smiled and said hello. "You're the guys Keiynan picked up this morning?"

I was chewing a bite of lukewarm pasta, so Jude answered. "He saved our lives."

Her smile faltered. Her name was Zaria, as we found out later in less peaceful moments. "It sucks out there."

"Not much better waiting up here," Kim added.

"I'd disagree," Keiynan said. "At least we're not being eaten up here."

"Fucking zombies," Kim said. "Real-life fucking zombies."

"There's gotta be more to it than that," Zaria said. "They're sick, but zombies? I still can't believe that."

"Have you watched one reanimate?" I asked. Kim, Keiynan,

and Zaria all looked my way. Jude chewed slower, looking down at his lap.

"I haven't," Zaria said.

"They're definitely zombies."

"But they're people before they throw up blood."

"They're just dying. They're taking as many people out with them as they can."

The wind was starting to pick up, and the clouds were getting darker. People were finishing their food and retreating to their tents. The sun was blocked by the clouds, but it wouldn't go down for some time.

"You guys had it rough out there," Keiynan said.

Jude nodded.

I clarified, "We watched five of our neighbors die today."

"So did the whole town," Kim said. "We should feel lucky we're not them."

I smiled. "You have a point."

"We should still mourn them," added Jude. "We can be thankful *and* sad."

Keiynan nodded in agreement. "Everyone here's lost people."

"My roommate tried to kill me," Kim said. "Tried to push me off our balcony. When I pushed her instead, I spent so long convincing myself it was self-defense—like I would have to tell a court. I doubt it."

Zaria leaned against Keiynan's shoulder. "Our mother lives alone," Keiynan said. "We tried to get to her, but her neighborhood was filled with them."

"Zombies," Zaria clarified.

Keiynan nodded. "I made the choice." Zaria hugged him tight. "I just hope she hid herself well enough." There were no tears on his face, but they were hiding right behind his deep brown eyes.

The food was starting to improve, tasting less like guilt and more like we might as well enjoy it because it was probably our final meal. For some, it would be.

A feminine scream echoed from close by. Keiynan got up, but Kim simply placed a hand on his forearm—not aggressively, just as a matter of fact. She shook her head. "It's coming from the apartment building. We can't go in there. There's nothing you can do."

"Is it that bad in there?" I asked Kim.

"Walking in is a death sentence. Everyone's infected, or they're a miracle."

Keiynan didn't sit back down until the screaming stopped. Then he quietly continued eating the wraps in front of him. If you listened hard enough, you could hear more sounds in the distance, sounds that I never remembered hearing in the town: moans and growls, faltering screams, and the silence of a lifeless sky.

Jude was still eating, but I couldn't anymore—not because I was full, but because it was beginning to taste like guilt again. I felt less like a person and more like a statue in a museum that you think could be watching you. My stomach was turning, like something was pulling out my intestines and eating them. You might ask: How did a person like you, an inconsequential and unimportant person like you, and not any of the other people you passed on the streets—how did it end up that you were led to safety? The answer: I have no fucking idea.

After dinner, we sat with Kim, Keiynan, and Zaria until the sun finally set, listening to stories from the night they'd had. People were everywhere—you would have thought it was rush hour—but they were fighting for their survival. People were attacking each other, dropping to the ground, spitting up blood, getting up and attacking each other again—just as we'd seen on the news. Those who decided to stay in their cars were ripped from their seats; those who decided to run were tackled to the ground by infected and bloodied ones alike; those who stayed home were interrupted not much later.

Jude and I walked back to our tent, but I paused at the entrance while Jude unzipped it; I looked out over the buildings below. We were four stories high, higher than most of the town, the whole suburb of Geyer a safe distance below us—for the moment.

Jude noticed. "Lyle, don't look over there."

I caressed his shoulder. "I have to." So I walked around behind our tent and leaned against the concrete wall that separated us from the hellscape below. An overpass was beneath us, a grassy field on top. At the opposite end of the overpass, fences lined both sides of the road. I could see where homeless people had set up a living room of sorts: two couches, a fire pit, a trash can, signs illegible at this distance. I wondered if they'd found a place to hide last night. (They hadn't. In fact, they were some of the first infected.)

Under the overpass, a man sat against the tunnel wall. There was just barely enough light for me to see the blood on his chest, dripping down his sides—dead or alive, I couldn't tell. Another man shuffled out of the tunnel. He also had blood on his collar. Off to the left, where Geyer's town center was, a tractor-trailer had been abandoned in an intersection, and down the road were some cop cars with their lights still flashing. I doubted anyone would return to them.

The man stumbling out of the tunnel looked up and saw me looking down at him. I couldn't see his eyes, but I recognized myself in his body—like a statue in a museum you think could be watching you, except he was certainly watching me. I pitied him and feared him. I feared the potential that he had; I feared him doing to me what I had seen done to Irene or Tina. I was next, wasn't I? Was it fate for me to die next? Was this all meant to kill me? Would it all stop once I met my doom?

The man below broke our stare and sprinted underneath me, out of sight. It wasn't the stumbling run of the earlier bloodied ones, it was a real sprint. I sprinted back past Jude, who tried to ask what was wrong, but I didn't answer. I ran down to the barrier where the two officers were still keeping guard.

"One's running up," I said.

And sure enough, the same man I had seen on the ground below rounded a corner and came running up the ramp towards us. The cop with the pistol, silencer attached to the barrel, took aim and shot, clean to the head. The one with the rifle turned to me and nodded. "Thanks for the warning."

Somehow, the bloodied ones were running faster. And we were quickly approaching the end.

# LYLE
*four hours prior*

**I**T WAS SUDDEN. How none of us expected it, that's beyond me—or rather, it was fucking stupid of all of us, every single one of us who'd found haven on the top floor of that parking garage. Was there anything we could have done? Maybe if we'd packed up and found a better place, maybe if we weren't squatting right next to a dam about to burst, or maybe if we hadn't acted so casually with a dying man among us. Alex was his name— the man lying in the infirmary tent. He was quiet, along with the rest of us, sleeping.

I woke up early in the morning. It must have been around four o'clock. It was still dark and still; the only sounds were bodies adjusting themselves against shabby tent floors over concrete and, if you listened closely, breathing. There were no more inhuman moans—it was like everything outside had taken time off or gone to sleep. Jude was shirtless and, where his warm skin met mine, it felt like we were burning, but it didn't bother him enough to wake him up. I tried to adjust, but footsteps—slow, heavy, approaching from the empty side of the parking garage—urged me to stop. The empty side—empty except for the infirmary.

I couldn't see outside the tent, but I followed the noise of the steps as they approached, boots on the concrete. I didn't move—I didn't want to wake Jude. I didn't want Jude to wake up and make noise himself, calling dangerous attention to what was inside our tent. I don't know how I sensed the danger. It felt like at that moment I had the ability to pick up on the slightest possibility of harm anywhere around us—*slightest* being a strange word when all possible harm was likely to occur.

The footsteps moved to the front of our tent and stopped. I prepared myself to fight, looking around for anything that could be used as a weapon. Jude's breathing changed; he was waking up. All of me wanted to say, *No, please don't wake up! Don't make noise!* And then the tent beside ours rustled. Were they waking up? Did they hear the noise? Or were they just turning over in their sleep? I don't know, but it was another lucky moment—for some. For us.

The steps outside shuffled into the other tent, not even opening the zipper, just crashing into it. We heard the rods of the tent snap and the fabric rip, and then the scream of a woman inside woke the rest of the garage, and the rest of town.

Jude shot up and grabbed onto me. I was already throwing his shirt towards him and pulling him up to get out. Our tent would be next at this point, no doubt.

"What's going on?" he asked.

"Run." I opened the zipper and ran past the collapsed tent. He was a bloodied one, and he had already torn through the fabric of the tent and the stomach of the woman inside. Her screams had stopped. Others were waking up and coming out of their tents as Jude and I were running past Keiynan, who was coming from watch at the barrier. He couldn't get to the scene before a shot rang out. Beside the crumpled tent, Luke held a gun, still pointed at the unmoving bloodied one. Farther down the wall, his child watched from inside the frame of their tent, holding onto the flap of the half-open door.

"What the hell, Luke?" Keiynan said.

"Don't even start, Keiynan!" Luke lowered the gun and turned to him. "You said you were going to keep an eye on that guy, and look what the *fuck* happened! And I thought you said he wasn't bitten!"

"He wasn't! We checked him."

"Then explain *this*." Luke pointed his gun again at the collapsed tent, the two dead bodies.

"I...I don't know!"

Keiynan didn't know, but in retrospect it isn't hard to figure out. Alex had a drug habit. He'd probably picked up the virus through a needle in some outdoor living room under an overpass.

"That guy could barely stand!" Luke said. "And *you* let him stay, and someone else got killed because of it!"

It was a political debate befitting the apocalypse, and just as quickly as it began it was cut short by the apocalypse. A gunshot from down by the barrier. Kim ran up the ramp leading below.

"Keiynan, we need you!" she yelled. "Everyone grab a weapon, there's—" Behind her, three bloodied ones came around the corner, leading the pack—then four, five, six, seven; they kept emerging. Kim drew her AR and shot at them, hitting two in the head before another leaped onto her, ripping through her shoulder. People ran out of their tents and away from the bloodied ones as Keiynan drew his own AR and fired into the pack, but for every one he killed, two more emerged. It was chaos.

Jude and I ran with the rest, but he stopped at a nearby scream. Zaria was trying to hold off another woman, a bloodied one, who was chomping at the air between them. Jude ran towards the thing, in some idiotically heroic adrenalin burst, and kicked it away from her.

I yelled, "Keiynan!"

He stopped firing and looked towards his sister, but it was too late: another bloodied one pounced into the space on top of Zaria. It bit into her neck. She screamed, her body squirming underneath the monster, this bloodied one ripping the life from her. Keiynan shot into the bloodied one's back, but that did nothing except make it twitch. The other bloodied one pounced at Jude, who held it away from himself, but it was strong and persistent.

"Jude!"

Keiynan fired another shot straight into the thing's head. It collapsed, away from Jude, who ran towards Keiynan as more bloodied ones converged on Zaria.

Another bloodied one (it was like a sea of the dead) ran towards me, but I ducked out of the way and sent it tumbling, only to have another catch me off guard and roll with me onto the concrete. I ended up on top, holding it at bay, calling "Keiynan!" to shoot it, and a shot came right into the bloodied one's head. It wasn't Keiynan, though; it was Luke standing above me.

"The stairs." Luke pointed. There was a clear path, but for who knew how long. I searched for Jude and found him following Keiynan the other way, down the ramp. He was looking back at me every few seconds.

I called out to him the first place I could think of, a place we could meet. "The drain!" I hoped he'd heard me, because I couldn't tell. I just hoped and ran alongside Luke, who shot the few that tried to run our way. On the second level, the stairs were blocked by everything you could think of. I pulled a desk from the barricade, a few chairs, a tire, a sign for the apartments, and a bike wrapped in a chain. One of the bloodied ones followed us into the stairwell, but Luke shot it down. We knew the noise would only draw more, so we shifted as many things as we had to for room to shimmy through to the other side.

The stairs led us out to the street on the opposite side from the vehicle entrance. It was quiet on this side, but there were still screams above us. "They came from the apartments," I thought out loud.

Luke didn't talk. He just stopped, leaned over holding his knees, and vomited onto the sidewalk. He was alone. His kid wasn't with him.

"Luke." I didn't know if I should be asking anything. His kid wasn't with him. He wasn't okay. There was nothing I could do. He vomited again. "Luke, I know where we can go."

It wasn't a crazy idea. The drain was relatively secluded, down a bike path and through a patch of trees that no one could really decipher, then over a fence to the pond on the other side. Lay low, I thought, and wait until Jude comes, and we can maybe find our way out.

The bloodied ones would be on us soon, searching for any strays. Luke looked up and aimed his gun at me.

"Shit!" I ducked, and the gun went off. I looked up and he had lowered it to his side. Behind me, a bloodied one was dead on the sidewalk.

"I'm gonna kill every last one of them," Luke said. "I'm gonna kill every single motherfucker up there."

"Luke, please. I need your help."

He was unmoved. Another bloodied one came out of the doorway. I moved behind Luke as he shot it down.

"Luke, we're going to die here. Please come with me."

Another came out and he shot it the same. Down the street, in the distance, there were more. They were sprinting faster than any of the newly reanimated. "Luke, we can't take them right now."

Luke held up his gun, looked down the barrel, breathed, and for moment I thought I would have to leave him alone. I wasn't going to die here when Jude would be waiting for me. I knew he would be waiting. I knew he was in good hands, and he was smart himself. I couldn't let him down. But then Luke lowered his gun. I breathed.

"This way." I smacked his shoulder and ran into a nearby alley.

Luke followed. We took alley after alley, then streets, then yards, then paths, keeping quiet and out of sight, slowly working our way towards the school.

# JUDE

*eight months after*

WORK WAS A place I could quiet my mind. The gym, less so, but it was something I felt Lyle could relate to; he always used to pester me to go to the gym with him. Maybe it was too late for that now, but better late than that he never see.

I visited him on Saturday mornings—except for the first weekend of the month, like this one, when visitation wasn't allowed because Dr. Cerrone and her team would be with him. Long, overnight studies of Lyle's infection. I hated first weekends. Part of me held out hope that maybe there was still a chance they'd develop a cure. But all of me was just upset they were taking more time away from us.

I went back to the locker room to change, as I always did. I was alone. It was early in the morning and not many people lived around here anymore. So many abandoned houses. I took off my shirt and glanced at myself in the mirror. I used to shudder away from my body in the mirror, but I stayed for a moment; my stomach was firmer now, my arms were tighter, and my chest was perkier. That's what Lyle had always wanted for himself: defined pecs. For once, I wasn't upset about seeing myself shirtless. There was something attractive about the way my V was deeper than I remembered, and suddenly I remembered the way Lyle used to run his hands down the V of my hips and...

I walked into the bathroom stall and pulled down my workout shorts. I was quiet, just in case anyone else walked in. I didn't take long at all, a minute—it had been a while—and afterwards I wiped myself clean, pulled up my shorts, and went out to finish getting dressed.

Always getting front row parking, looking both ways before crossing the road back to the parking lot and not seeing another person, car, or soul in any direction—hey, at least there were no corpses—that was the experience of staying in town when most others had left. It's a miracle any businesses were still open, but government grants dedicated to "revitalizing the community after a disaster" kept them there—in a community that had mostly packed up and gone. Why did Lyle and I stay? At first, we believed we could return to normal; redesigning our home would put everything behind us. We thought we could really rebuild something, together, but then Lyle got sicker, and I don't think either of us wanted to change anything about the small amount of time we had left.

I sat in my car for a while; I didn't want to start it. I was sick of going home to a quiet house, so I scrolled through Facebook on my phone. It's funny how the rest of the world had all but forgotten about the outbreak; the only time it was mentioned anymore was to criticize the president's reaction to it, how slow he was to send in the national guard, the doctors, the scientists, anyone!

Social media only made me more upset, but I was still scrolling through my feed when a message request notification came up. People were always reaching out, especially after Lyle's story went viral, but I didn't have the patience or stamina to keep up with it all. I opened up this message anyway: it was from Keiynan. Up until that moment, I'd been suppressing the memory of Keiynan quite successfully—him and everything else about that forty-eight hours.

> **Keiynan:** *Hey! I know you're busy and under a lot of stress, but I'll be around Geyer this afternoon and was wondering if you'd like to meet up. Coffee?*

I hadn't spoken to Keiynan since quarantine and didn't know where he'd gone off to. I only knew he hadn't stuck around town. He'd kept saying he wanted to get as far away as possible from Geyer. But most other nations wouldn't let any Americans across their borders until months after the country was declared infection-free—until the military had conducted a house-by-house search, until all the survivors were found and contained, until after a period of extensive testing and research. Keiynan had been long gone by then. I was curious about where he'd disappeared to and how he'd ended up back here. But mostly, I figured he might need a friend as badly as I did.

*Jude: I'll be around. Coffee sounds great! What time?*

*Jude: It's nice to hear from you.*

I added that last part on a whim, because it was very nice to hear from him.

*Keiynan: Any cafes still open?*

*Jude: Starbucks on Main Street. What time?*

*Keiynan: I'll be there at 3.*

It was easy to spot him. Keiynan looked exactly like he had when he saved us—which had happened right down the street from the Starbucks. He sat alone at a window-side table, sipping from an iced coffee, the afternoon light glistening on his skin. His face was shaved clean, his hair grown out a bit since he'd left quarantine. He smiled when he saw me. We said hello, I ordered a caramel iced macchiato for myself, and we sat down to talk.

"You've been gone a while," I said.

He nodded. "To California. It was nice there, except the beach is a lot colder than you think."

"Why did you come back?"

"I missed my family." We paused. I studied him. "You're still wondering why I came back," he suggested.

"No, no." My body shifted in the seat. "Are you staying with someone?"

He shook his head. "I got an apartment outside the city."

I knew what he missed. Keiynan missed the dead. He missed being near his family, and there was nothing he could do about it. "I'm sorry about Zaria and your mom."

"At least they're together," he said. "California was weird. Every time I met someone new they immediately asked me where I was from, which is apparently pretty normal. I tried to keep it vague—the East Coast, something like that—but they usually put it together. Something like, *Oh, were you near the outbreak?* Yeah, pretty close. *How close?* I was in it. After that, they treat you like you're infected. Not that I blame them."

"You should see how the nurses treat Lyle." I smiled. There was something pleasurable about being able to one-up him. "When you're actually infected, they run for the hills, or at least quit their jobs."

"Any chance we can visit him?"

I shook my head. "He's not allowed visitors this weekend."

We talked for a while about California and all the odd jobs Keiynan did to make ends meet: office assistant, waiter, Uber driver. He usually kept where he came from a secret to avoid striking fear in the hearts of the ignorant. We lived in a little bubble—right now it included the lone barista behind the bar, a woman reading a book on a cushioned chair, Keiynan, and me—where it was okay to have lived through the outbreak. We were all just trying to forget it as fast as possible, while living with the remnants.

"I left the area once they released us," Keiynan said. "I didn't even go back home, or to my mother's house. God, what kind of guy doesn't go back to his mother's house when she dies. I just got on a bus and headed west. Nothing was holding me back, right?"

I nodded. "I'm sorry."

"Don't be sorry. I was running away from everything, but I'm back now. If anything, I should be saying I'm sorry to you. I can't imagine what you're going through."

I produced a bogus smile. "It sucks."

"I imagine that much." He raised his empty cup. "I'm going back to my mom's house tomorrow, packing everything up into boxes and shoving them in my truck to sort through in my tiny apartment. It's not going be a lot of fun." He laughed, like you have to laugh when the most gruesome thoughts come up. "But if you want to wallow in someone else's misery for a change, I wouldn't mind having you hang out there a bit."

I grinned suspiciously. "Are you asking me to help you move?"

He laughed again. "You don't have to touch a single box if you don't want to. If you can't see Lyle this weekend, though, it's at least an excuse to get out of the house. Not much else to do around here, is there?"

I looked around the mostly empty Starbucks, remembering when the place would have been packed at this hour. "Message me the address and we'll see."

Keiynan smiled. "Like old times. Fighting the ghosts together."

* * *

After Lyle and I were separated at the parking garage, I escaped with Keiynan in the truck. He wanted to keep driving. I screamed at him to turn around, *turn around or I will crash this car immediately*. He was unresponsive, mourning the death of his sister, but I knew—I knew somewhere so deep and spiritual—that Lyle was still alive, and he would meet me at the drain.

Keiynan pulled over on an empty residential road. He got out of the car and held his face in his hands. He was crying, but he wasn't just crying. He was sobbing. He was breaking apart on the sidewalk. He was so loud I worried more about attracting unwanted attention than I did about his sanity. But I cared enough not to just take the truck and go. I sat down next to him and held him, letting him sob into my chest, and then I lifted his shoulders. "Keiynan, we need to go to the high school. Lyle will be there, I know it. He's quick, he knows his way, and he's more than resourceful."

After a bit more crying, Keiynan got back into the driver's seat, I followed into the passenger seat, and we turned around.

But by the time we got there, it was too late.

Keiynan's mother's house was painted yellow with a matching yellow lawn. It was one story, with faux-muntin windows and a beige-shingled roof that extended over the narrow, cracked, and weed-infested driveway as a carport. Matching properties lined both sides of the street. It was almost the American dream: perfect and quiet and wholesome. But everyone on the street was dead.

Keiynan and I started packing up anything we saw of value (monetary or otherwise) in any box that had room. He said it didn't matter what went with what, as long as nothing broke; he would just go through it all later. I felt some vicarious pain at packing the legacy of a dead woman into boxes. Was it Keiynan's pain? His mother's? Maybe both. Or maybe it wasn't vicarious at all. Maybe it was because I would be doing this one day for all the people I loved, or they'd be doing it for me.

Keiynan kept coming inside and resting against a wall or cabinet, watching me lift a box before resuming his own packing. I was starting to get annoyed with him, thinking he was using me for some kind of free labor, but then he leaned against the couch's arm and watched me lift a box with a small television, some DVDs, and a couple of miscellaneous cords.

"Did you start working out?" Keiynan asked.

I smiled. "It's something to take my mind off everything."

"Your arms are more toned than I remember."

You know the term *butterflies in your stomach*? When Lyle goes through an episode—which has been happening more than once daily—he'll throw profanities my way. I try to forget them. One day, when he was strapped to the bed—he had already learned that fighting against the straps was pointless—I said I loved him and he called me a faggot. He was so calm I couldn't determine if it was part of an episode or an expression of his true feelings. "You're such a disappointment," he said. "How could you let this happen to me?" He stared at me and didn't blink even when his eyes began to dry and glaze over. Not crying in front of Lyle was becoming easier—as easy as holding back a reservoir of water with your bare hands. I didn't let him see how much he'd hurt me, but in that moment I felt my stomach drop and twist and deform. One simple, subtle compliment from Keiynan, on the other hand, given almost the way Lyle used to talk to me, released thousands of butterflies I didn't know were still inside me.

We kept packing countless boxes and stacking them in Keiynan's truck. We had shoved all of the living room and kitchen into boxes by hour four, which was most of the house, but many of those boxes still needed to get shoved into the dwindling space in Keiynan's truck. I suggested we tackle the bedroom next, and Keiynan reluctantly agreed. The smell is always different in someone's bedroom. The rest of the house smelled like dust, but her room had kept the scent of lavender. Keiynan smiled when he walked in.

He opened the blinds of the small window by the bed, letting strips of light into the room. The bed was still made, possibly remade early on the morning of the outbreak, or maybe never slept in that night. Keiynan opened the closet where her clothes dangled. He moved over to the bedside table and picked up a small picture frame, smiled, and invited me over.

We sat on the edge of his mother's bed. I looked at the photo. A young boy with a huge grin sat on the house's front doorstep beside an even younger girl with short hair. "That's Zaria," Keiynan said, "and that's me."

I smiled. "She kept it by her bedside."

He nodded and sat on the perfectly made bed. I sat beside him. His grin was much smaller now than in the photo; after everything he'd been through since it was taken, his face had grown heavy and his smile conservative. "I'm happy I came back to say goodbye," Keiynan said. He wiped a tear from his cheek. "Why does family have to do this to you?"

"It's their job. And it's our job to take it. Could you imagine if no one missed you?"

He shook his head. "What if we're the last ones, and there's no one left to miss us?"

I shrugged. "Either we meet them in heaven or there's no way for us to care, right?"

"Which do you think?"

"We'll meet them in heaven."

Keiynan placed the frame back on the table exactly as he'd found it. We sat in silence for an eternity, or at least what felt like one. Keiynan looked at me. His stare was inquisitive.

*Lyle, I'm sorry.*

I leaned towards Keiynan, like I had no free will in the matter, but it would have been my choice regardless. His lips were bigger than Lyle's, soft like clouds. I kissed him delicately, and then he kissed me harder, his hand touching my arm, but guilt set in. The butterflies were gone, and my stomach was falling in on itself. I pulled my face away.

*Lyle, I'm so sorry. It didn't mean anything.* But it did.

"I liked that," Keiynan told me.

"I think I should go." I got up from the bed.

"Wait." Keiynan followed me into the hallway. "I'm sorry, I know that's—I mean..."

"It's okay." I stopped at the door. "I did it. I just have to go." And I did.

Keiynan messaged me on my drive home, telling me to call him if I wanted to talk about it later. I didn't. I only wanted to talk to Lyle. About it? I don't know. I wanted to be with him, but I couldn't that night, so I went home and lay in my bed. The hours slipped by, the light got thinner, the room got darker, the quiet got silent, and suddenly I couldn't even feel the beating of my own heart anymore. Had it stopped? What if I died before Lyle, and he would only have to mourn me for a little while before we found each other again?

When I walked into Lyle's room, he sat in the corner chair, a blanket over his lap, reading *Station Eleven* by Emily St. John Mandel. He was rereading some of his favorites. "God forbid I read anything new and my last reading experience be horrible!" he told me.

He looked up when he heard me say hello. He smiled. His smile was sunlight.

"Do you mind if I finish this chapter?" he asked.

"Go ahead." I fixed the covers on the bed while he read, then sat down and aimlessly picked dust from the comforter. As Lyle's become calmer in his episodes, he's become calmer outside of them too. Part of me wanted that, some sense of control being established, but part of me couldn't shake the feeling that he had given up.

Lyle set down the book. "So how was your weekend?"

My eyes flickered between his chest and the floor below him. "Lyle, I need to talk to you about something."

He grabbed the blanket on his lap, scrunched it into a ball, and threw it to the ground; he leaned forward. "What's wrong?"

"I did something stupid." I was looking at the bed covers again, picking off more of the dust. I could barely even mumble the words.

"You slept with someone."

I looked up from the bed. Lyle was emotionless—not sad, not happy, not angry; not an episode, not calm, but more like the version of himself he used to be. I had to tell him, and the only way I could do it was by a hesitant shaking of my head.

He paused, then guessed again. "You kissed someone."

"Yeah."

"Who?"

"Keiynan."

He was surprised but not angry—composed, like he'd been expecting this.

"Jude," he said. "I understand, and I'm not mad."

"I am."

"Don't be."

"How can I not be?"

"It's been eight months, Jude. Practically forever." He was still on the edge of his chair, a little melancholy creeping into his demeanor. "Don't you want a break from taking care of me?"

I shook my head. "Don't say that. I love you."

"I love you too, but I'm not going to be around much longer."

"You're my husband. I made a vow and I'll be there until—"

"I want you to have something for yourself that survives, Jude."

The bare branches of the lilac bush tapped against the window, then slid back and forth in the wind like claws scratching the glass. We sat with only that sound between us.

"Go out with him," Lyle said.

I looked at him like he was crazy. "Why would you tell me that?"

"Because you like him."

"I don't! I love you! We're married."

"And I'm giving you permission to go out with him."

I shook my head.

"Do you plan to never fall in love again?" he asked.

I tried to answer in my head, then tried to answer with my mouth, but it only opened and no words came out, and no thoughts came clearly to my head, but I kept trying.

"I want you to," he said. "You should."

"I don't want to think about that."

"Don't, then, but *talk* to Keiynan."

"Stop!" I sprang up from the bed, ruining the neat covers. My hands found my thighs and rubbed off invisible dirt. I wasn't living this life; I wasn't having this talk. Lyle was quiet. He leaned back in the chair, pulling his legs in. "Can I talk to you tonight?" I asked.

Lyle nodded.

And I left.


I left his room but stayed in the home. I talked to the coordinators and begged for every last bit of pity they could offer us. How many times do those employees have to listen to family members beg for things and use the excuse that their loved one is dying? Everyone there was dying. But Lyle was a special case to them—the first ANA patient in a nursing home—so they all knew him, and they all knew me, and I guess that earned me a little bit of extra pity because they let me do what I had planned.

That night, one of the nurses—a broad-shouldered, middle-aged man—escorted Lyle to the garden. The spring air was still chilly, so he wore a sweater, and I waited for him on the other side of a dinner table laid out for two—a folding table with a tablecloth and two folding chairs. Lyle smiled when he saw the extravagance, trying to hold back a laugh, but he giggled anyway. The garden was mostly lifeless, but the breeze gave life to the bones of the plants. The sun was gone; dusk was over. Lyle sat opposite me. Candles lit both our faces. The nurse walked back to the garden door and kept watch from afar.

"What is this?" Lyle asked.

"Lemon chicken over rice."

"Can you make anything else?" He looked at me seriously. For a moment, I feared it was the dawning of an episode, but then he laughed it off. He was kidding. "I love this."

"I'm so sorry, Lyle."

A breeze came through and his hands receded into the sleeves of his sweater. His arms folded over his stomach. "You have nothing to be sorry for."

"Yes, I do. And this isn't my apology, it's my way of saying I'm *starting* to show you how sorry I am."

Lyle watched his food like it was spinning, following some invisible runner around the rim of his plate. "This is the most beautiful thing anyone has ever done for me," he said. "This is the reason I love you, the reason I'll never stop loving you, and the reason I'll find you in the next life and love you all over again.

"But—" he looked up at me "—I need you to promise me you'll go on a date with Keiynan. Promise me you'll try to have a good time. And promise me you'll let whatever both of you want to happen just happen and don't think that I'm against it, because I'm not."

I shook my head. "I can't do that, Lyle."

"Do you like him?"

"I love you!"

"They can both be true." He paused. The nurse was watching us closely. "Jude, we haven't had sex in five months."

"I know, and that's okay—"

"It's not okay," he said. "I think about it every time I tell you I hate you, even though it isn't true—it's never been true.

But it's always what I want to say in that moment. You don't deserve to get that every single day and not have some sort of happiness in your life."

"*You* are my happiness."

"Some sort of *consistent* happiness." The nurse was coming over. Our time was up. "I love you, but promise me you'll try."

"I can't."

"Jude, I need this."

I looked up at the nurse coming over. "Just one more minute, please."

He nodded and backed up to lean on a tree a short distance away from us.

"Jude, please."

I swallowed hard. "You can't expect me to love someone else."

"Not right away, but tell me you'll give it a chance."

All the dead flowers around us in the garden were listening. Winter was holding on this year, but the flowers were waiting, just waiting. I thought to myself: *Who is this for? For me? For him?* Or maybe it was for *us*, and I just couldn't connect the dots yet. "Okay," I told him. "I'll try."

Lyle smiled. "And I need you to promise me something else."

I nodded.

He leaned closer to me so he could whisper. "Promise me you'll buy a gun, and promise you'll bring it here every time you come to visit, and promise you'll never tell me about it and never let me get my hands on it."

"Why would I—"

"You know what it's for, Jude. I've made peace with the inevitable."

There's protocol for his final moments: all theoretical, of course. If Lyle is alone in his room when he turns, his steel door will remain locked until Dr. Cerrone and her team arrive. *We'll put him down humanely*, that's what she told me when Lyle wasn't there to listen. If Lyle is outside his room, in the hallway or in the lobby, the building will go on lockdown, and everyone will either be locked in their rooms or locked out into the courtyard until the agent from Dr. Cerrone's team stationed out front can come in and put him down humanely. If Lyle is out in the courtyard, the lockdown is reversed. On the other hand, if it's just me alone with Lyle in his room, I'm supposed to get out as fast as I can at the first sign of the change. *I know it will be hard. It's hard even talking about these kinds of protocols, but Lyle wouldn't want you to get hurt, so if you see him start to vomit, leave the room, lock the door, and call the nurse immediately. When my team gets there, we'll take care of the situation in a safe and humane manner.*

But Dr. Cerrone doesn't know Lyle as a human being, only a patient and a research subject, and she definitely doesn't know me.

"The doctors said—"

"Matt." Lyle turned to the nurse. "I'm ready to go inside." He turned back to me. "I love you so much."

"I love you too." I couldn't bring myself to smile at him, but I meant every word.

"Sleep well," he said. "Dream good things tonight."

I sat there while Matt took Lyle inside. Neither of us had touched the food. I moved our plates to the ground, folded the tablecloth and table and chairs, and watched through Lyle's bedroom window as Matt let him in and locked the door from the outside. Lyle's eyes met mine and he smiled. He looked so beautiful then, young, spirited, like nothing was wrong except he was tired. He blew me a kiss. I caught it, then he got into bed.

# JUDE
*nine months after*

KEIYNAN RESERVED A table far away from the outbreak, an hour south, in a town deep in Delaware. On the ride there we tried to make small talk, the kind of small talk that people who know each other like we do usually don't have to make.

"How was your day?"

"It was okay. How about yours?"

"Some errands and such, but not much else."

There was a brown tint to the restaurant—leather chairs, cedar walls, wooden tables, high seats against a red-lit bar. It was classy. It was dreadful. But Keiynan looked so nice in his blazer that I didn't have the heart to tell him how dreadful I thought it was. This place was for the middle-aged and frivolous, frivolously throwing money at steak and younger men or women. We could not have become that already.

We were seated at our table. We tried to talk about other things besides the way we'd met; we had agreed we would learn more about each other than just our shared horror. He liked baseball. He'd joined a recreational baseball team during his time in California. He listened to more Taylor Swift than he liked to admit—so did Lyle, but I decided not to bring that up, to let it sit there on the outskirts of the conversation.

We got our food, some fancy steak that I wasn't used to or especially fond of. He shared stories of his time in the "desk military." I told him all about college, brushing by Lyle, or trying to. Eventually, though, the thought of Lyle grabbed onto me, like it was him during an episode, holding me, sinking his teeth into me.

I felt it coming.

I have this memory from when I was no more than ten years old. As a child, I couldn't fall asleep unless one of my parents was still awake, usually my father watching television. Whenever they were both asleep and the house was silent, I felt frozen in my bed. I cried because I didn't want monsters to get me. When I was younger and I cried, someone would come into my room to check on me—my parents or one of my sisters—and knowing someone was awake helped me sleep. That's all it was—wanting to know that someone was awake with me, someone was there. Later on, they were slower to peek in. One night, it was ten o'clock, no one was awake, and I cried. I cried because I felt there was no other way to express the fear of dying alone in my sleep, the monsters getting me while I sat awake and the rest slumbered. I cried because it was the birthright we all receive to tell our mothers we're hungry or tired or terrified of the past, present, and future. But that night, no one came.

"Jude, are you okay?" Keiynan asked.

I started to cry like a child, because no one at home was awake anymore for me to go to sleep to the sound of them living.

"Jude?" Keiynan got up from his chair and crossed over to me, kneeling beside me. I was crying—no, I was sobbing, and people were watching, both the waiters and others having dinner. "Jude, what is it? Talk to me."

I felt bad for him, because it was nothing he'd done and there had been no warning. I just missed Lyle. I missed the days together we had lost, the lifetime, because the monster under the bed that I was afraid would take me away when I was six years old was now taking him.

"Maybe we should go home," Keiynan said.

I tried to compose myself, I really tried, but it was no use. Everything was out in the open. Keiynan paid the check and we left. I had gotten it together a little more by the time we started driving, but Keiynan still let me be.

"Are you upset?" I asked once we got on the highway.

"Of course not. I'm just confused."

Keiynan had an ornament of a surfboard dangling from his mirror. It bounced around as the engine shook the truck. The truck wasn't the greatest, but it had been through hell, so it had its excuses.

"I promised Lyle I'd try," I said, "but I don't think I can."

"Try what? To date me?"

"Yeah."

"I understand." He was quiet as he merged into the next lane. "I'm sorry. I might have gone for a little too much tonight."

I chuckled. "That place was horrible."

"Hey! That's the best steak in the tri-state area."

"Lyle and I were burger people, maybe with some mac and cheese on the side. Our favorite spot was Applebee's."

"We have different taste, you and I."

Keiynan drove slowly and cars passed us frequently. He didn't have a radio in his truck, so there was no music.

"So, you said you joined a baseball team in California?" I asked.

"Yeah," he said. "We were the Rogers, named after..."

We talked like that for most of the ride home, changing the subject when things got stale but keeping it light. I gave him the directions to my house. When he pulled into the driveway, I took a moment to look at it: such a big first home for some-one my age. It was too big to stay in alone.

"Do you want to stay over?" I asked.

His eyes got wider for a moment. "I'm not sure that's a good idea."

"Not to do anything," I clarified. "I just don't wanna be alone."

He nodded, understanding as much as he had to, and fol-lowed me in. I pulled a pair of sweat pants from my dresser and gave them to him outside my bedroom, and he walked down the hall towards our spare room.

"Wait." I stopped him in the hallway. It wasn't anything I'd thought through, more something my heart was telling me to do. "Do you want to stay in my bed?"

He looked at me from the other end of the hallway, startled. Then he nodded and walked back to my room. I sat on the bed as he changed his pants, facing away from me; his boxers were loose around his thighs but tight around his butt, his leg hair light but abundant. He slid on the sweatpants.

We lay beside each other, on our backs, both of us obviously still awake ten minutes after laying down. The wind was heavy outside, whistling against the windows. It was supposed to snow that night, but as far as I knew the ground was still clear.

"Jude?"

"Yeah?"

"Would it be okay if I held you?"

Would it be okay? I asked myself. Lyle's voice was telling me yes. "Yes."

Keiynan rolled over and wrapped his arms around me. He was warm, and our bodies moved closer together every time we shifted. It was comforting to have someone else in the bed again, to sleep beside someone I cared about. I woke up the next morning with his arms still there.

# PART FOUR

*The Lilacs*

# LYLE

*three-and-a-half hours prior*

**W**E WERE LUCKY, that's the only thing I can say—as lucky getting out of the garage as we were getting safe passage into it in the first place. Luke and I made our way into the back streets as quickly as we could, avoiding the bloodied ones along the way. Luke wanted to shoot our way through the business district, but we only had three bullets left, so I restrained him. We found our way to a residential neighborhood. I needed something to defend myself with as well, so I picked up a piece of broken wood from a trash can left out on the curb. It was a good thing Luke had saved the bullets, because as we cut across a backyard to access another road, a bloodied one came out the back door of the house. Luke missed two shots, hitting its head on the third. We kept running after that, trying to put some distance between us and the sound.

Not many people used the bike route on a normal basis, so I suppose it made sense that the bloodied ones didn't show up along the trail, through the patch of wood, or around the drain. Luke stuck his handgun in the crotch of his pants, gripped the chain-link fence, and started climbing. I followed much the same way, but without a gun in my pants. The concrete was the same as I remembered it: littered with debris, weeds, and cigarette butts. As I placed my feet on the ground, I couldn't help but wonder if any of these were mine, standing the test of time.

"Why here?" Luke asked.

I shrugged. "It came to mind. It should be kind of safe." I looked across the pond and the parking lot to the school that appeared abandoned, like it did every summer. There were no roamers, no blood, no guns, weapons, or bats; there was only the faint nostalgic sense of comfort. The sky was a definite blue—last night's rain had dissipated and revealed the sun. I think people who say the weather controls them, like clouds mean they're going to have a bad day, are full of shit. I was staring at the sun and I was still in hell.

All of me had hoped Jude would be waiting for us, but we waited at the drain for an hour, minutes ticking by like years of lost life, and no one showed up.

"What are we building a society for anyway?" Luke sat against the fence, his back to the forest, the town, and everything else. His eyes had been closed for about ten minutes. I thought he had fallen asleep. I couldn't think about sleeping or anything else but pacing and watching the path through the trees for any sign of Jude. Luke didn't seem to care. I'm not sure he cared about anything. He unbuttoned the dress shirt he wore, exposing his hairy chest to the sun. "We spent thousands of years building this shitty world, only to have it taken apart in a day. ANA. ANA is the bitch of nature taking it all away."

"Luke, I'm sorry."

"For what?"

My eyes lowered. "I'm sorry for everything that got taken away from you. Nothing about that was natural."

"Do you think ANA was made in some lab?" Luke asked. His eyes were still closed. His face was pale. I thought he didn't look so well, but then again, I probably looked like shit too.

"I have no idea."

"I bet it wasn't. ANA was made by the world, and we're gonna die because that's what the world wants, I guess."

"Fuck that," I said. "The world can fuck right off if that's the plan."

"Don't use that language in front of my kid."

I looked at him. He sat alone, his eyes still closed, but he smiled, like someone was resting on his chest. The sun was all over his face; I worried it might burn him, but he didn't seem to care.

"Luke." I couldn't think of anything else to say.

"I love you, Carson." The comfort he seemed to take from the inside of his eyelids was off-putting to me. I clenched the broken piece of wood in my hand. "Mommy's gonna be all right. She's gonna be there too, and Pop's gonna be there and Nan and Daddy. We're all gonna be there." His smile faded.

"What? No, Dad's not going anywhere, kid. I'm gonna be right here. No, no one else is here, bud. No more monsters." His face contorted like someone had told him the most appalling thing. "Daddy's not gonna be a monster, bud. No, no, Mommy wasn't a monster. Mommy wasn't there. Carson, listen to Dad and stop talking. Mommy was not there, you're lying. Daddy won't be a monster, now go to sleep. Daddy's not a monster. Stop screaming. Stop screaming, Carson. *Carson, stop screaming!*" He screamed the last bit himself.

I was scared of him drawing any more attention to us. "*Luke.*"

Luke opened his eyes, and they focused on me like rifles. "Go to sleep, Carson."

"Luke, he's not really here."

Luke grabbed the fence to help himself up. "You think I don't know that?"

"I'm sorry, it's just we have to be—"

"No, you have to be quiet while I talk. That's how this is going to work. It's okay, Carson, Dad's going to handle it."

"Luke, why don't you sit back down, and I'll just leave you alone."

"Do *you* think I'm a monster?"

I didn't answer, only tightened my grip on the stick.

"You think I'm a monster."

I thought he was insane.

He stopped moving around, as if the whisper he was looking for had led him to me. One shoulder slumped more than the other. The blood on his hands matched that on his thighs. His bare chest rose and fell in heavy breaths. His upper lip twitched. His eyes focused their guns on me. "I'm not a monster."

"Luke—" But I couldn't say another word before he lunged at me. I ducked out of the way and ran to the other side of the fenced-in area. Luke drew the gun from his pants, but there were no bullets left. He lunged at me again. I tried to move away, but he smacked the barrel of the gun into my leg, sending me stumbling to the ground. On the next lunge, he clobbered my shoulder. He hit me again and again until I flipped over onto my back. He straddled my waist and tried to bring the barrel down across my face. I reacted in the only way I could think of: this was how I could save myself. I gripped the wood and shoved it, broken point first, into his stomach. The jolt that went through my body when it pierced his skin was terrifying, more terrifying than the barrel of his gun coming towards my face. The gun slipped from his hands and onto the concrete. The wood didn't go all the way through him, but it wouldn't come out when I pulled, either. Luke fell off me onto his back.

I scrambled up to my feet and watched him straining to breathe. "Kill me," he said, "or I'll kill you and everyone you've ever loved."

For a moment, I lost all my pity and grabbed the wood and pulled it from his stomach with all my strength. He was still taking shallow breaths. The pity quickly reemerged, reanimated like a bloodied one. It was ravaging me. My stomach was turning worse than his looked.

Luke pushed weakly against the concrete and sat up. I kicked the gun away from his hand, but when I did, he grabbed my leg and pulled. I lost my balance and fell to the ground again. He pulled himself onto me, dripping blood onto my clothes. He placed his hands around my neck. I swatted him away, but he kept trying. His weak hands wouldn't give up. I pushed him off of me and stabbed him again with the wood in the same spot. I stabbed again in a different part of his stomach—another hole that was hard to pull the wood from, but I did, and I stabbed him again, and again, and again. He wouldn't die. He was coughing, close to death; his face wasn't angry anymore. He looked sad. I reminded myself that he would never stop attacking me, that I was doing what I was supposed to do. I stabbed him again even though every part of me was begging me not to.

Finally I stopped and threw aside the bloodied wood and slumped onto the ground beside Luke. He was dead. His face bore a faint remnant of terror. Blood pooled beneath him.

I walked over to the edge of the drain. I sat down, legs hanging over the water, and stared at the school. Now *that* would have been the perfect time to light a cigarette. I felt the need for a cigarette, the need to wash everything off, the need to wake up and realize this was all just a dream. I squeezed my eyes. "Come on, come on." I was awake. I had been awake. I had killed a man.

A bloodstained hand gripped my shoulder. I shuddered and flung it away, but a whole body followed to push me off the drain. I lurched forward, falling into the dark, shallow water below. Two bodies fell: mine and another's. My head slipped under the water, the water slipped into my nose, and I felt hands grasping my arms and thrashing around with me. I swung my head out of the water but couldn't open my eyes. I kicked the attacker off me. When I rubbed the water off my eyes, I saw Luke, his face washed clean, his collar stained, his eyes glazed and red. He pounced on me, pushing me backwards into the bottom lip of the metal drain. My vision went fuzzy, the ring of the drain vibrating inside my head, and I tried to shove Luke away again, but I felt a burning sensation on my forearm. I kicked and thrashed some more until I'd beaten Luke back enough to make him fall, and then I crawled inside the drain.

I crawled through the stagnant, murky water, back towards a dark abyss I couldn't differentiate from the darkness of the metal walls. Everything was still fuzzy. I turned around and watched Luke rise again from the water, stepping into the drain. This was the fate I wouldn't escape. *Jude, I'm sorry.*

"Lyle!" I heard his voice, his sweet voice, tinged with fear. Maybe he could hear me after all. *Jude, I love you.*

The drain rang again, echoing the sound of a gunshot, vibrating my head like an earthquake. Luke fell into the stagnant water. Two more bodies appeared outside the drain, both running towards me. "Lyle!" It was Jude again. Jude was there, standing over me, holding me in his lap. "Shit, shit, his arm!" His voice was muffled, but I could make out the words. I looked at my arm, and I could make out enough of the picture to tell I was bleeding. It was a bite mark. *Luke, you bastard.*

Keiynan stood over us. "What do we do?"

"Lyle, it's gonna be okay. It's gonna be okay."

But I knew it wasn't. It was an easy fate to accept. I wanted to go to sleep right then anyway, so maybe I could just not wake up. Maybe I could break this cycle of dying and killing, *dying and killing again*.

"Jude, I love you," I said.

"I love you too, now you have to stand up."

I heard another voice, but it was neither Jude nor Keiynan speaking. It was distant and outside the drain. I was about to pass out, so I couldn't figure out anything at that point. Part of me was even okay with them leaving me there if it meant Jude could survive. I was ready to go to sleep, and if I survived somehow then anything after that would be borrowed time.

Everything I know after this is from Jude, my partner, my love, my other half. Perhaps Jude can better tell the rest.

# JUDE

*minutes after*

THE STAGNANT WATER inside the drain was quickly filling with Luke's blood. I held Lyle in my arms.

"Jude, I love you," Lyle said.

"I love you too, now you have to stand up." I tried to help him up, but he was limp. Was he dying already? Had he hit his head? I was terrified to know the answer.

"Is someone there?" a voice called from outside the drain. Keiynan raised his rifle at the opening. "National Guard. Please respond."

Keiynan looked at me. I looked at Lyle, whose eyes were flickering. "We're in here!" I called. "Help!"

The troops were there in seconds, pointing their weapons at us. There were two at first, then two more came inside the drain with their guns raised. "Don't move," the woman said. She asked Keiynan to hand over his weapon.

"I'm retired Army," he said.

"Disaster protocol."

Keiynan didn't fight.

The other man checked Luke's corpse, flipping it over with the barrel of his rifle.

"Please help," I said.

"When was he bitten?" the woman asked, pointing at Lyle's arm.

"Just now," I told her, even though it could have been earlier. I hadn't been there for him.

"Hendricks," she called to a man standing guard at the front, "help me get him up. Radio alpha base."

"Are you sure?" he said. "What if he turns?"

"We have orders," she said. "And it takes longer than that." She turned to look down at me. "It's your lucky day."

# JUDE

*eleven hours after*

WHEN LYLE WOKE up, I was sitting beside his bed, an actual infirmary bed in an actual infirmary tent. A soldier was in the tent with us, standing guard at the door. Two of the other beds were occupied by people with injuries I couldn't identify; all I could tell was they'd been through hell too.

Lyle's eyes flickered open. "Jude?"

"I'm here," I told him. I wove my fingers through his hair.

"I'm infected." He was so objective, like the knowledge that he was going to die wasn't even a bother.

"Not anymore," I told him. "They got antivirals into you after you passed out."

Lyle let his head fall to the side, his cheek against the pillow. He closed his eyes again, like he'd accidentally woken up too early and was going back to sleep. He smiled. "Is this a dream?"

"Nope," I said. "We can't go home for a while, though. They keep doing tests on you."

Lyle examined the bandages wrapped around his forearm. "Where are we?"

"A National Guard camp," I said. "They set up around the firehouse."

A middle-aged woman came into the infirmary tent. Her lab coat was stained along the bottom seam, and her hair was wrapped up in a hazardous black bun. She had exhaustion shadows under her eyes and her brown skin was ashy, but she smiled when she saw Lyle awake. Her name was Dr. Cerrone: head of the international research team studying the ANA virus. She'd sat down with me as soon as we got to the camp, as soon as they separated Lyle from Keiynan and me. She'd explained to us that they had been testing antivirals. It was all medical talk, stuff neither Keiynan nor I could fully understand, but it helped to know they were doing everything they could.

"You're awake!" she said. "Is your head okay, Lyle? You got a pretty bad concussion this morning."

"How long has it been?" Lyle asked.

"About nine hours," Dr. Cerrone said. "Jude's been insistent about staying by you whenever he can. You have a good partner."

I smiled. I had been quite *persistent*, to say the least. But Dr. Cerrone was there to calm me down, along with Keiynan.

Keiynan was dealing with his own loss. Now that the camp was quieter, he had the time to sit down and mourn. Anytime I couldn't be with Lyle, I was with Keiynan to listen as he cried. Sometimes that's all a person needs.

Dr. Cerrone sat down on the other side of Lyle's bed with a clipboard, examining notes. "You don't have the urge to kill anyone, do you?" she asked.

Lyle shook his head. "Maybe myself." We both looked at him with disappointment. "I'm kidding," he clarified.

"Well, we have all your blood tests back, and it looks like your viral load is dropping at a steady pace, so I would say the antiviral treatment was a success.

Lyle smiled and turned to me. "Can I hug you?" he asked.

I nodded and reached into the bed. He squeezed me tight, cracking my back.

"It's as much a relief for the world as it is for you," Dr. Cerrone said. "We were hardly ready for something like this on a bigger scale."

I kept hugging Lyle, squeezing him back until he was out of breath.

We stayed in that base for weeks, and then they gave Geyer an all-clear. News of the successful treatment spread around the world even quicker. A vaccine was developed in a matter of weeks—practically overnight as far as vaccines are concerned—and the world breathed easier.

But it wasn't over. Soon, "survivors" started to show symptoms of stage one: aggression, loss of control, lungs filling with blood. Dr. Cerrone's team went back to work, and what they found was that the antivirals had only killed *most* of the virus. While the vaccine was effective, once the virus was in you—as Dr.

Cerrone would describe it to Congress when questioned on her team's biggest failure—"This thing is fucking invincible."

The treatment had extended victims' lifespans, but the virus was still there, festering inside their blood. It was gnawing slowly at Lyle's brain.

"The hardest part," Dr. Cerrone would later write in her memoir, "was telling the families how long they had together."

# JUDE
*ten months after*


THE LILACS SPROUTED, the magnolias bloomed, the dead-nettles budded. The primroses are thriving and everything outside Lyle's window is flourishing again. The garden of Winterbury Village is well taken care of by the staff. The leaves have been coming in on my last couple of visits, as warmth takes over the East Coast so quickly you don't even notice it until you're stuck in seventy-degree weather with jeans and a sweater. Other patients are out in the garden—some I recognize from looking out Lyle's window last year; some are new, and there are some notable missing persons, like the man who would sit on the bench in a robe, grinning at the sun.

Inside Lyle's room, the lights are turned off because they were hurting his head. The doctors say his episodes are becoming less frequent, but his health is failing. They have to drain his lungs every few days, but that's only a temporary fix. He's spending a lot of time in bed, his head on the pillow but his eyes open and awake. He looks pale, paler than ever. We are reaching the end.

"Jude, can I ask you something?"

I stand over his bed. "Of course, babe."

He asks, "Have you been happy recently?"

"Life could be better."

"But have you been happier than before?"

"I don't know what that means."

He sighs across the pillow, his temple still firmly pressed against it. "Will you be okay when I die?"

I have asked myself the same question. *Will I be okay when Lyle dies?* I won't be happy, but I've been anticipating the mourning process for so long now that it feels like I'm a child again, listening to my father watch television and knowing I'll never fall asleep. I'm listening for the inevitable moment when my father goes to bed without saying good night, and then I start crying for help even though I really *really* don't want to bother anyone. I know I have to, and so do they.

"I'll be okay," I tell him.

Lyle smiles. "Good." He pauses. "Does Keiynan treat you well?"

I sit down in the chair beside his bed, putting my hand through his hair to massage his scalp. "We don't have to talk about him."

"I want to," he says, a little aggressively.

I nod in submission. "Keiynan treats me very well. We went out again last night."

Lyle grins. "Did you do it?"

I roll my eyes. "No, we didn't. We haven't done anything."

"Well, that's dumb."

In truth, I told Keiynan I wasn't ready to do anything sexually intimate with him. I told him I didn't think I would be ready until sometime after Lyle passed. That's how I've been referring to it recently: "passing" instead of "dying." It's easier to say.

"I think you can love him and still love me," Lyle tells me.

"Why do you think that?"

He looks up at me. "Do you remember Danny Bridges?"

"Yeah." Danny was the boy we talked about in high school, the boy he saw for a while, the boy he talked about hating during college.

"I never stopped loving him. Maybe not the same way I love you, but there was potential. I could be wrong, but I think love is on a different level than friendship. Once you start loving someone, you can't go back to that friend level, but you can love someone in different amounts, the same as friendships. I'm not afraid you'll ever stop loving me, and I don't think you should be afraid, either."

I bring the palm of my hand around to his cheek. "So, what you're saying is you think I might love you less, once you're gone? Because that's not true."

"No, not at all," he says, "but you'll love me differently, and that's not either of our faults."

"Are you okay with that?"

Lyle nods against the pillow. The nightlight plugged in below casts a soft glow against his face. He closes his eyes for a moment, then reopens them. "Jude, can you get me a lilac from outside?"

The window is a subject of great debate between Lyle and the nurses. "You want me to—" I overdramatically pause. "*Break the rules?*"

Lyle frowns. "Just open the goddamn window."

The aggression doesn't bother me. I kiss Lyle's forehead. "Yeah, give me a second."

Lyle sighs. "I love your kisses."

I open the window. I search through the few lilac branches I can reach to find one that is at least mostly in bloom. The sky is cloudless, the sun is bright, the lilac branch is hard to snap free. I twist and bend until I get it to snap halfway and have to pull off the rest. I end up getting more branch than I wanted to, but I settle for that as long as I have the flowers.

I close the window and turn around.

Lyle has turned the other way, and the picture that's been repeating in my head like a daily nightmare matches too well. "Lyle?" I ask for his attention. He doesn't respond.

I notice he's not breathing. I drop the lilacs on the floor and walk around the bed. Lyle lies with his eyes half-open, his temple resting against the pillow, his mouth dripping blood, his arm limp in a pool of that blood. I've imagined it a thousand times before now.

I go pick up the lilac branch, placing it on the chair in the corner of the room. I lean into my bag on the floor, into the pocket behind my notebooks and other work materials. I keep it there only when I come here, because of a promise I made to

Lyle. The nurses have never searched my bags, and I don't know what I'd say if they did. *I haven't brought this to kill my husband, I've brought this to kill what he'll become. Because that's the promise I've made, and my responsibility. And I'll accept the consequences.* I sit across the room from him, lilacs in one hand, a handgun in the other.

He doesn't reanimate as fast as the ones we've seen before, as fast as Terry or Tina or Luke. It takes him almost half an hour—I almost believe he won't reanimate, but that would be too easy. I use the extra time to work up my courage, to appreciate the fucking pointless poetics. To a God that would do this to us for the purpose of poetics, fuck you.

Lyle gags and finds the motion of his body. He finds every limb by twitching and kicking slowly, eventually pushing the covers from his body. He turns in the bed, his glazed eyes meeting mine. He doesn't look like Lyle, because he's not Lyle. He's the husk he fades into during his episodes. The episodes are over, and this is him in his entirety. This is the monster that's been tearing apart my husband and tearing apart me.

It pulls my husband's body head-first onto the floor. As much as I love Lyle, I have no love for this thing coming towards me. It pulls itself to stand, jaw hanging loose, shoulders slumped, the whole side of its body soaked in red. I stand up with it, leaving the flowers behind. I hold up the gun. "I love you, Lyle."

The bloodied one lurches at me,

and I fire.

# LYLE

*one year prior*

**I DIDN'T HAVE A** best man at our wedding; instead, I had a maid of honor, because fuck gender roles and fuck the traditional wedding. Carly was my maid of honor, and she helped me get dressed. She smoothed out my maroon suit, brushed my hair (I insisted I didn't want it styled in any special way), and even put on a bit of makeup to cover the pre-wedding breakouts. She called me beautiful, and I thought I looked pretty damn good. I could only imagine how beautiful Jude would look.

One part of a traditional wedding that I did want was us not seeing each other until we were at the altar. I wanted to see him for the first time at the ceremony and smile as hugely as I knew I would. I wondered if he was having the same jitters I was about getting married, but then again, what was the big deal? We were practically married before he proposed. Still, something about a wedding, confessing your love in front of everyone, sharing your lives, taxes, and *insurance* with each other was daunting. Okay, yes, it was definitely the joint financial situation that was daunting. Loving Jude was the easy part.

Our wedding was held outside a banquet hall. Dusk was just beginning, the sky was orange, and guests from among our families and our friends were claiming their seats under the gazebo by a small lake surrounded with flowers. It sounds like such a typical wedding, and that's because it was a typical wedding in more ways than not—but it was *our* wedding.

Jude walked down the aisle first, his mother on his arm. When he got to the altar, I finally got the cue to head down the path. My mother held my arm. "Are you excited?" she asked.

"I know I'm a dick sometimes," I told her, "but thank you for raising me well."

She laughed. "You're welcome, Lyle."

My mother walked me up the aisle. Every face was looking at me, but I only saw one, the most beautiful face in all the world. Jude was stunning, wearing a new suit and his favorite pair of glasses even though the loose screws on the left side made them fall down his nose. He pushed them up and smiled my whole way to the altar. When we met in front of the minister, she began a ceremony that was just religious enough to please Jude's family and just modern enough to please us. When it came to our vows, I went first.

"I've spent a lot of nights recently wondering how much of our individual lives could be considered part of our shared experience. How similar is my inner world to yours? Jude, when you look at your past, you see a childhood spent in drastically different ways than mine—some better, some worse—but you also see a boy who used to lay in bed and wonder about the same things I did, and we still do: How do we create meaning in our lives? Is art really truth? Will the plot of *Kingdom Hearts* ever make sense?" A small minority of the audience laughed; it sounded mostly forced. "I can't promise answers to those questions. I can answer something else, though. How much of love is a common experience? Will we experience love the same way as everyone around us?" I looked up from the paper. I looked at Jude's ocean-blue eyes. "No. We'll experience it personally, together, with our own path of hardships and beautiful moments—maybe only minutely different from our neighbors', but just for us. We'll have a marriage filled with more of those moments, but we'll also have a partnership filled with love. You've shown me nothing but love.

"Jude, I promise to love and respect you forever. I promise to care for you and tease you for always. I promise to be there for you, as you will for me. Jude, I love you."

The crowd's reaction wasn't important. Jude was smiling, and that's all that mattered, although the crowd didn't disapprove, either.

"Lyle, you know I'm not much of a writer," Jude began, reading from his paper, "but you insisted on writing our own vows anyway. I can't follow up the vows *you're* inevitably going to write, but I can make a few promises. First, I promise to love you forever and even after that. I promise to express my feelings to you and encourage you to express your feelings in the same way. I promise to keep our living space clean, because I know you hate it when things get too messy. I promise to be there when you need me, no matter how late you call or how weird and unexpected it gets. I promise to be by your side from this point in our lives until the end. And one last promise. I promise to promise more things as our relationship grows and changes and we grow and change with it. Lyle, you are the love of my life, and I promise that's true."

Our first dance was to "Weathered" by Jack Garratt, a song we listened to frequently during college. One night, as we sat in a parking lot before I dropped him off, we'd listened to the song. That was when Jude leaned on my shoulder and told me he loved me for the first time since we got back together.

That's the thing about love: it's messy. It builds you and breaks you and makes you question everything about yourself, but you never hold any of that against your partner. You don't push it onto them as a problem; you ask yourself how you're going to change—if you *want* to change—to be a better you, to have a better relationship, to love and be loved in the way you want.

It's strange having everyone watch you dance. I never realized how much family we had between us—how much support.

One hand draped around his neck, the other in his palm, I leaned in, and I whispered in his ear, "I promise I'll always love you as much as, if not more than, I do now." That was a promise I would always keep: in this life, in the next, forever.

# ACKNOWLEDGMENTS

T HANK YOU TO MY WISE, supportive, and truthful editor, Christine Neulieb, for seeing the soul of this story and always helping me make sure it came through. Your mastery of words breathed color onto my black & white pages. And thank you to the entire Lanternfish Press team, you are all-star warriors.

Thank you to my mom, for so much love it makes me cry of happiness in a Mexican restaurant on my third margarita with a sombrero falling off my head (you know the photo). And, of course, thank you to the rest of my family, for always keeping me grounded in suburbia.

Thank you Rowan University, for pushing me to create and giving me the confidence to put my work out into the world. Specifically, thank you Dr. Drew Kopp & Dr. Liz Hostetter.

And thank you. For letting me speak this long.

## ABOUT THE AUTHOR

**MATTHEW VESELY** collects ironies. Usually, he's scribbling in his journal while somber music plays in the dark. But when you meet him, he's more likely to be giddy talking about new books, reality TV, or dogs. Striving to portray real queer experiences through the lens of fiction, he lives, works, and writes in the Philadelphia area.